COMPLICATED PAST

A BAD KARMA SPECIAL OPS NOVEL

TRACY BRODY

ONE

Poland

WATCHING the Ukrainian team's sniper trip and fall to his hands and knees, Staff Sergeant Linc Porter's entire body clenched. In combat, that mistake could be fatal. What happened next, though, made him interrupt the exercise.

"You *never* leave a man behind," he barked at his squad of soldiers.

"He can't keep up. He'll get us all killed," one of the young Ukrainian trainees complained.

"He's the best marksman on your team. You need him. Would you want your team leaving *you* behind if you twisted an ankle and were the slowest man?"

Two of the younger soldiers glanced from each other to their older teammate. "No," they admitted.

"Right. We're going to run this exercise again and then again." Until they understood this was a team and each man had worth.

If they didn't gel as a team, they would *all* end up dead.

"I can't believe we'll be sending these troops into the field in two weeks," Dev said.

He voiced the thought that also went through Linc's head as the men regrouped to practice today's infantry tactics training exercise.

The men on Linc's Bad Karma team each had over a decade of experience and highly specialized training. That's how they'd earned their spots on one of the most elite units in the US Army. However, his team only had two months to impart what they could to improve these men's chances. Few of these men had any military experience, but they stepped up to serve because they were motivated to protect their homeland. However, they didn't have the skills or equipment needed to adequately defend their country or their lives.

Half the men were in their mid-thirties or older. Two hadn't managed to complete the ten-mile ruck. Several of the men still couldn't make it over the five-foot wall on their own. And now they were willing to sacrifice their own team members.

The grim reality was that many wouldn't come home to their families.

Linc signaled for them to begin again. "It sucks we can't do more." Except it wasn't their war. At least not yet.

It took the US nearly two decades to withdraw from the Middle East, and watching the Taliban sweep right back in and negate so much of what they'd done there didn't sit well with any of the men on the Bad Karma team. The US sent troops over to train the Ukrainian military, but Washington wouldn't risk committing to another war where they weren't assured a victory. That limited his team's involvement.

Chief Lundgren dismissed the men after a ten-hour day turned into nearly twelve hours. No point exhausting everyone to the point they wouldn't retain what they learned.

Linc and Dev joined the rest of the team and headed to their temporary quarters at the Polish military base. Accommodations were not quite on par with the barracks when Linc had gone through basic training at Fort Jackson twelve years ago but were still a step up from his numerous Middle East deployments in the past decade.

Once inside the cramped bunkroom, half his teammates called their wives and significant others. Linc saw he had a missed call and message notification from Brianne and did a double take. He'd managed to tick off his sister again before he left for this deployment, so they'd only talked when he initiated calls. Maybe this was a good thing. He could hope.

"Linc, I did something stupid and don't know what to do. I'm—"

A woman spoke over Bri, drowning her out before the call ended abruptly.

Shit. Something stupid? What this time? His gut constricted as his mind immediately went to the obvious. He replayed the message. Bri didn't sound strung out, but her low tone wasn't normal. The best he could make out, the other woman asked who she was talking to. While Bri might not want her co-workers overhearing, something about the other woman's tone pinged Linc's radar.

Though it'd been nearly two hours since she left the message, Bri hadn't called back or texted. Maybe she'd figured out how to handle whatever it was. He couldn't count on that, so he hit the call button. Seconds later, the call connected but went directly to voicemail. "I got your message and wanted to check in. Call me back. Tell J-man Uncle Linc says hi. Love you both."

He drummed his fingers on his leg. Maybe Bri emailed him. He checked. Nothing from her there either. She was a grown woman. Since completing rehab, she'd gotten her life together with some help from him and a lot of motivation from Jalen. In that way, she was different from their mother.

Please don't let her backslide. There wasn't much he could do from halfway around the world. His limbs hung like weights, and swallowing didn't dislodge the lump in his throat.

"Everything okay?" Dev asked as the team headed to the mess hall for dinner.

"Not sure. I got a message from Bri saying she'd done something stupid," Linc confided.

"You thinking she relapsed?"

Dev knew his sister's history. Hell, the whole team knew. "I'm hoping not. I didn't reach her when I called, but I'll try again later."

"If you need, Stephanie can check on her." Chief Lundgren's gaze fixed on Linc.

The chief's wife headed up the Family Readiness group, but that might be beyond the scope of her responsibilities. Though they'd met, having Stephanie show up at Bri's door when she had already accused Linc of being overprotective wouldn't go over well. He was trying to trust her, but with their past, it was damn hard to let go of the need to protect her. "Thanks, Chief. I'm sure that won't be necessary."

His calls after dinner and an hour later went straight to Bri's voicemail. It wasn't like his sister to have her phone off for an extended period. Along with what she'd said and the other woman's voice, Linc couldn't let this go, especially when each unsuccessful attempt sent his thoughts to darker and darker places. He tried a fourth time, then pulled up the website for the dealership and connected to the number for the service department before they closed for the day.

"Can I speak to Bri Porter?" he asked the man who answered.

"She's not in. Do you need to schedule service?"

"Has she left for the day or . . .?"

"I think she's out this week."

"I needed to talk with her." It's not like she had to run plans past him, especially with him being deployed, but her being out for a week didn't sound like Bri, even if she had been on better financial footing since starting this job. Combine it with her saying she'd done something stupid, and the unease tickling the back of his neck sunk its claws in to hold on tight. "Put me through to her voicemail."

Bri had updated her message to say she'd be out of the office for the week. The message sounded normal, which eased his mind that Jalen was all right. But Bri reaching out if she was in trouble, despite him not being there for her in the past, left Linc with few options. He left her a message on her work line, then set an alarm, hoping to get hold of her in the morning.

LINC MANAGED to get some sleep but woke in the night twice due to nightmares. He hadn't had a nightmare this bad since before their mom and Bri's dad died. Still no texts, calls, or emails from her. He didn't care if he woke her calling at nearly eleven her time. Better to piss her off and know she was okay so he could focus on his mission here.

The call went to voicemail again. She wouldn't have blocked him. Not after that initial call. Unless she'd really screwed up and wanted to get her head on straight before talking to him.

He waited until the rest of the team woke before tapping Devin. "Can I borrow your phone? I want to make sure she hasn't blocked me." His buddy handed over his phone without hesitation. Linc tapped in the number, hoping for different results.

Voicemail.

"Shit." He hung up and handed the phone back rather than listen to the message.

"Still haven't connected with your sister?" the chief asked.

"Not yet."

"Play the message for me," Lundgren requested.

Linc pulled out his phone. Getting non-biased feedback could give him some peace of mind and direction. The team crowded around in the kind of support he needed. He hit play, closed his eyes, and listened to Bri's voice rather than study his friends' faces. He clung to the hope that he was overreacting. Though replaying Bri's message still made his muscles tense, knowing his team had his back helped him breathe.

"Play it again," Tony Vincenti requested. Vincenti did most of the team's undercover work and excelled at reading people and situations. "She's speaking low like she doesn't want to be heard, and I don't know her, but the distress in her voice is real. Do you know the other woman talking?"

"No clue who she is." The woman sounded young, maybe mid-twenties. Despite the southern accent, her harsh, unprofessional tone didn't sound like a co-worker or Bri's boss, who Linc recalled being male.

"Does she sound under the influence to you?" Vincenti asked.

"No. Just scared." If she were high, she wouldn't have called him to confess when he was deployed.

"I agree," Dev said.

The heads bobbing in agreement lessened his fears about her using drugs but didn't banish his gut instinct that Bri was in trouble.

"Let me know if you need *anything*." Chief Lundgren held eye contact until Linc gave an affirmative nod.

"If Stephanie can call the preschool and make sure Jalen's there and go by Bri's apartment, I'd appreciate it." He hadn't anticipated this with how well Bri had been doing.

After breakfast and four hours of training, where Linc struggled to concentrate, the men broke for lunch. Linc waited for Chief Lundgren to finish a conversation with a Ukrainian officer before he approached. "Any word from Stephanie yet?"

"She called the school and managed to get confirmation that Jalen's in class. Then she went by Bri's apartment. No one was there, and nothing seemed off."

Between the message Bri had left Linc and not being able to reach her, this news wasn't enough to reassure him. *What's going on, Bri?* "Would Stephanie mind going by again tonight?"

"I can ask. There's also a flight back to Fort Liberty leaving at fourteen hundred hours. I'll sign off on emergency family leave."

"I'd hate to leave the team short-handed, but—"

"No buts. It's family. You're all she's got."

That wasn't entirely true. She had Jalen, the reason she'd turned her life around. But addiction was a powerful thing. What would happen to Jalen if Bri backslid? Linc knew—and he wouldn't let that happen to his nephew. "I'll be back as soon as I get things straight at home."

"I'll let them know you'll be on the flight. Keep me updated. Dismissed."

"Thanks, Chief." Emotion choked Linc that Lundgren had already checked on flights. He breathed easier, though he had no idea what he'd be walking into once he returned to Fayetteville, North Carolina. However, the chief letting him go so easily reminded him that while he was an integral part of the team—which was as much like family to him as his sister and nephew—he wasn't replaceable. There were dozens of men who trained and worked equally hard who would love to take his place. Regardless, he needed to be there for Bri—he owed her that.

TWO

Fayetteville, North Carolina

THANKFULLY, Kendra's phone finally stopped ringing, so she didn't have to continue talking over it to answer the prospective foster parents' questions. "We do have foster parents who take temporary placements on short notice," Kendra explained. "Typically, you're given the child's history and why they are in foster care before you agree to a long-term placement."

"Would we know up front if adoption is a possibility before accepting a child into care?" Charlene asked.

"Yes. Is that your hope?" While reuniting children with their families was the goal, in situations where that wasn't a possibility, the ideal outcome for a child was a permanent placement with a family willing to adopt.

"It is." Charlene answered without hesitation. Her husband placed his hand over hers. "Unfortunately, several rounds of in vitro didn't work for us. We looked into adoption, but we can't afford to go through a private agency. Friends at church mentioned foster care to adoption, and we think that's the path we're meant to take."

"That's great to hear. Are you open to older children?" Kendra eased into giving them realistic expectations if they had their hearts set on a newborn or infant.

"Considering our age, we think a toddler or preschool age would be a good fit." Charlene's gaze flicked toward Kendra's purse as her phone rang for the third time in the last five minutes.

"I am so sorry. Let me check this." Telemarketers and spammers weren't usually this persistent. Seeing Bright Beginnings Daycare on the phone's screen likely meant a problem with one of her clients. "I'm afraid I need to take this."

"Go right ahead," Charlene said.

"Kendra Andrews."

"This is Rachel Davis at Bright Beginnings Daycare. Sorry to bother you this late, but no one has picked up Jalen Porter today. According to his teacher, Brianne's out of town. A relative dropped him off, but she's not answering the number Brianne gave us, and neither is Brianne. We tried calling his uncle, listed as the emergency contact, and can't reach him either. I've had Jalen in my office for the past hour hoping to hear from someone, but our procedures require that I notify Brianne's case worker—or law enforcement."

"I'm glad you called me. I'll head there right away," she promised and ended the call. It wasn't solely the terrible timing that twisted her stomach in knots. Not showing up wasn't like the Brianne Kendra had come to know serving as her case worker. She also knew Bri's history—and that history settled on Kendra's chest like a two-ton weight.

"I am sorry to do this, but I'll have to reschedule to complete your interview," she told Charlene and her husband. "I promise I'll make it as soon as possible."

Charlene escorted Kendra to the door. "I hope everything works out."

"Me too." Now, she had to figure out where she could place Jalen. Hopefully, on a temporary basis. This didn't make sense. Bri was one of the success stories. She was off probation. All her drug tests had been clean. She'd moved up to a customer service representative at the car dealership where she worked. Maybe the person watching Jalen was confused about the pick-up time or had been in an accident. *Please let there be a reasonable explanation.*

Kendra pulled up to the curb at the daycare, which specialized in providing early intervention for children with developmental delays. As she exited the car, a woman with long, brown hair exited the building and locked the glass front doors. She led Jalen over.

"Hey, Jalen." Kendra bent over to get closer to his level. "I'm your mom's friend. Do you remember me?"

His adorable face scrunched as he shook his head.

"That's okay. I remember you had a stuffed dog. What was his name? Tanner?" Kendra tried to remember to establish some trust.

"Champ! Uncle Linc gave me him for my birfday."

"Yes. You showed me Champ when I came to your apartment." A plan started to form. "You said Bri was out of town. Do you know where?" she asked the director.

"I don't. I can check to see if she told Jalen's teacher."

"Who brought you to school today?" Kendra asked.

"Grams."

"I wrote down the contact name and phone number Bri

gave us on the authorization to pick him up." Rachel handed Kendra Jalen's backpack and a sheet of paper.

She looked at the name on the paper. Regina Feldman.

If she remembered correctly, that was Bri's grandmother. How old would that make Jalen's *great*-grandmother? She'd pull up Bri's file and verify that. Also listed was Linc Porter's number. The soldier who'd gotten his sister into rehab after her arrest.

Kendra hadn't seen him since they'd met when he'd been at Bri's when she came to do the home inspection. However, Bri had brought Linc up. Usually, complaining about him acting like an overprotective dictator. Kendra understood he cared about Bri staying clean and out of trouble, probably so he didn't have to keep coming to her rescue, but she'd rather not have to deal with the alpha soldier. He likely felt the same after what happened before.

"Do you have a booster seat?" Rachel asked.

"I do." One of the job's requirements, even if she didn't have kids of her own—yet.

"Jalen, it's okay to go with Miss Andrews."

He settled onto the booster seat, and Kendra fastened him in. The older Jalen got, the more he resembled his uncle. Same brown eyes and soft brown skin color. Similar facial features, though she didn't know if Linc had a dimple. Jalen's smile was all Bri's.

"I hungry," Jalen said.

"Me too. Would you like chicken nuggets or a hamburger?"

"Chicken nuggets and French fries." His face brightened.

Perfect. She knew where they could eat, and he could go to the play area to buy her more time to reach Bri, her grandmother, or her brother to avoid entering Jalen into the system.

"We'll see you tomorrow," Rachel said.

Hopefully. Kendra closed the car door. "If you hear back from anyone, have them call my cell. I'll take Jalen to my office and try to reach them again before I find a respite care placement."

THREE

Linc powered his cell phone on when the C-17 touched down. Taking the military transport beat waiting for a commercial flight and making connections to Fort Liberty, but it wasn't set up for comfort. There was no inflight food service, internet, charger ports, or entertainment for him or the other two passengers bumming rides back to the States.

He'd stretched out the best he could and maybe dozed off for an hour or two. Not enough. Nervous energy flowed through his body like touching a low-grade electric current as he took his phone off airplane mode. Immediately, it pinged with voicemail notifications. He'd be pissed if he'd bagged out on his team and flown across the ocean, only to land and hear everything was fine. Still, he'd happily take that over finding that Bri had relapsed, or worse, overdosed and was in a hospital or morgue. He'd run through all the worst-case scenarios, hoping to prevent them from coming true.

He hit play without checking the call record. Instead of Bri's voice, he listened to the director of Jalen's daycare program telling him that Mrs. Feldman hadn't picked up Jalen from school.

His pulse picked up—not in a good way. He tamped down his personal feelings about Regina Feldman.

It made sense that Bri would ask her grandmother to help with Jalen, especially with Linc deployed. But where would Bri have gone that she wouldn't take Jalen with her? If she'd gone to Atlanta to see her old *friends*, she'd have dropped Jalen off at Regina's. God, he hoped Bri hadn't fallen back in with the crowd she'd run with there.

The next message, also from Rachel at the daycare, said she'd have to contact the Department of Social Services if no one came for Jalen in the next half hour. *Crap*. She'd left that message close to two hours ago. He skipped to the last message and stood as soon as the huge aircraft came to a stop.

"Mr. Porter, this is Kendra Andrews with DSS. I'm your sister's case worker." Like he'd forget her? "I picked up Jalen from the daycare and am taking him to dinner. If you get this message, please call me as soon as possible. I—"

He hit the callback button without listening to the rest of the message. "This is Linc Porter," he started before she'd finished saying hello.

"Uncle Linc!" Jalen called out his name over the speaker phone.

Thank goodness she still had Jalen with her. It sounded like they were in a car. "Hey there, J-man. You okay?"

"I want Mommy."

Linc wanted Bri too. "How about I come get you?"

"O-kay."

"Where can I meet you, Ms. Andrews?"

"I was headed to my office—"

"Let's meet at Bri's apartment instead. I can stay there with Jalen." While he figured out where Regina was. And why Bri had left. And where she'd gone. So many questions he needed answers to.

Kendra paused before speaking. "That'll work."

"It'll take me about twenty minutes to get there." *If* base ops got the message that he'd be back and transported his car from the storage lot to the airfield. If not, he'd call for a ride. Whatever it took to keep Jalen out of the foster care system.

LINC PARKED a few spaces from an occupied car in front of Bri's building. A woman got out and opened the back door. In the dim light, he recognized Kendra.

"Uncle Linc!" Jalen sprinted to him.

Linc caught him mid-leap and hugged him to his chest for several beats before joining Kendra.

While she still had a nice, curvy figure, she looked thinner than he remembered, though it'd been roughly four years since he'd seen her. She also didn't smile at him, not that he could blame her, considering she was still working at nine at night. She handed him the child-sized camouflage backpack he'd bought Jalen for school. Linc's gaze flicked to her bare ring finger on her left hand.

He shook it off. She was not why he was here, and she'd blown him off when he asked her out giving some lame excuse about a conflict of interest, being Bri's case worker. By that point, she knew his general history as well as Bri's. If anyone should understand and give him the benefit of the doubt, he'd thought a social worker, and one who, like him, was multi- or bi-racial wouldn't hold his past against him and dismiss him as unworthy.

"You aren't going to write this up in Bri's file, are you?" he asked.

"Technically, she's out of the system, but I'm supposed to document this. If you had called me sooner—"

"I called you the second I got your message. I was on a plane over the Atlantic."

"Oh." Kendra broke eye contact and swallowed. "Where is Bri?"

"I'm not sure." Totally clueless. "I've been on deployment in Europe." He didn't tell her about Bri's frantic message about doing something stupid. That *would* go in her file, and he wasn't doing that to her or Jalen. "Her work voicemail said she was out of the office for the week. Jalen, do you know where your mom went?"

The boy nodded right in Linc's face.

"Where?"

"A trip."

Not helpful, not that he expected much from a four-year-old. Maybe there'd be some information in the apartment.

He didn't see Georgia plates on any cars parked near Bri's building, though Regina might have flown up. Then she would have needed Bri's car, which he didn't see either. "Let's go see if Grams is here." He set Jalen on the ground.

"Are you coming wif me to see Champ?" Jalen took hold of Kendra's hand.

"Yes, you promised to show me."

Great. Linc had planned to say goodnight and goodbye right here. He didn't know what he'd find inside Bri's apartment. What if Kendra found something to warrant taking custody of Jalen?

"How old is your grandmother?" Kendra asked Linc, following him toward the building.

"She's not *my* grandmother." And she had let him know he wasn't a blood relative after his and Bri's mother were killed in the auto accident with Regina's son, Clifton, driving while stoned out of his mind. "But I'm guessing she's at least in her mid to late seventies."

"Is she in good health?" Kendra's tone clued Linc into what she was thinking.

"I think so."

As they climbed the stairs, a knot formed in Linc's throat. He might not like Regina, but he didn't want to find her lying on Bri's floor. She might still act fearful and avoid eye contact with him, but the few times he'd been around Regina for things like holidays and Jalen's birthday parties, Jalen had changed her perspective. At least she'd accepted *him.*

He knocked on Bri's door, hoping it would miraculously open to Regina or, better yet, Bri. The second time, he pounded harder. He tried the knob. Of course, it was locked. He pulled his wallet from his uniform pocket and removed his lockpick set. Dropping to a knee, he inserted the two picks into the deadbolt.

"You can't break into her apartment," Kendra protested.

"Yes, I can." A tumbler fell into place. "I'm on the lease, so technically, it's my apartment too. But I don't have a key on me." He didn't elaborate that Bri had taken away his key and accused him of not trusting her ability to take care of Jalen. He'd bought food at the post exchange and dropped it off at the apartment to help her out. It's not like he had anyone else in his life to spend money on. But, growing up the way they had made her independent to a fault. That's why he didn't take her reaching out to him lightly.

The last tumbler clicked, and he turned the bolt. "Wait outside with Jalen while I check the apartment."

"Good idea." She held Jalen back, even though he whined about wanting his mom.

"Just a minute, J-man."

Linc did a quick canvas of the inside. Everything was in order. A suitcase sat on the floor in Bri's bedroom with clothes that had to belong to Regina based on the blouse he examined.

Bri would never wear the collared shirt with a large floral print pattern.

The bathroom was clean and empty. He checked the trashcan—no signs of drug paraphernalia. Though Bri would know to dispose of that someplace safe and where it wouldn't be discovered, the tightness in his chest lessened.

Jalen's room was empty, and the twin bed was made. He scooped up the stuffed Golden Retriever toy he'd given Jalen before returning to the front door. "All clear."

Jalen took the dog. "This is Champ." He held it up to show Kendra.

"Nice to meet you, Champ." She played along.

"Go put on your PJs." He steered Jalen toward his bedroom, then took the backpack from Kendra. "I'll stay with him tonight." And maybe start calling hospitals. "Thanks for picking him up, but I've got it from here."

"It's not quite that simple," Kendra started. "With what happened tonight, there are procedures I need to follow."

Shit? Really? "I'm his relative." No way was he letting her put Jalen in the system. Linc's core tightened as he prepared to battle to keep Jalen with him.

"That will make it easy to appoint you as his temporary guardian until we get in touch with Bri. If you can come to my office in the morning, we can do the paperwork, and I'll get it signed off by the magistrate."

"Fine. What time?"

"I'll be in the office between nine and eleven. And you'll need to undergo a drug test."

"Seriously?"

"It's standard protocol in situations where there's a family history of drug use. It's not my rules."

He knew all about generational addiction. It was why he'd *never* done illicit drugs. He was not following his mother's path. It haunted him that Bri had. "No problem. It will be clean." A dirty drug test could cost him his spot on the Bad Karma team. "And if Regina shows up before then?"

"Bring her with you. We'll test her too."

While he didn't expect Regina to be using, the idea of making her undergo a drug test reduced the tension by a degree. But she would have to explain herself before Linc would trust her with Jalen.

FOUR

After getting Jalen to bed, Linc searched the apartment for clues on where Bri had gone and found nothing. It only took him a few attempts to guess her passcode on her laptop, but no emails provided clues.

He called her number, and it went straight to voicemail—again. Trying not to sound pissed, he left her a message that he was in Fayetteville and had Jalen. None of this made sense, and despite his growing unease, he didn't want to alarm Jalen.

With his mind still coming up empty, he crashed in Bri's bed. If Regina showed up and found him there, he'd vacate—after giving her an earful.

He woke to his alarm and no Regina at dawn. Still no texts from Bri either.

He mixed up pancake batter before he woke Jalen.

"Is Mommy home?"

"Not yet." He didn't even know when she was supposed to be home.

"Where's Grams?"

"I don't know, but I'll find out," Linc promised. He'd already made a plan and action steps to start once he dropped

Jalen off at school. He scrambled eggs to go with the pancakes and added extra chocolate chips to make a smiley face on the top one for Jalen.

While he'd only taken his nephew to daycare a handful of times, he knew the routine and drop-off time. Getting there early should give him an opportunity to talk with Jalen's teacher. Then he'd go by the police station, take a damn drug test, and jump through whatever hoops he had to for Jalen's sake.

KENDRA TOOK a breath before exiting her office to greet Linc. She hadn't heard back from the messages she'd left both Bri and Regina last night or the ones this morning. At least Linc was here and stepping in for Jalen, even if he wasn't her biggest fan. Just as well. Seeing him in uniform last night was the reminder she needed to avoid military men.

This morning, he wore well-fitted, faded black jeans and a simple black V-neck tee that clung to his body like it wanted to show off all the muscles it hugged. "Any updates?" she asked, trying to project a dispassionate professionalism.

"Jalen's teacher said Bri mentioned going to Mexico with a friend. But she didn't know what city or who the friend was. And Mexico? I don't know how she'd pay for that. If we can contact her grandmother, Mrs. Feldman, she should know more. I called the local hospitals, but they didn't list her as a patient. Before coming here, I went by the police department and filed a missing person report."

"Best not to wait. Did they put out a silver alert?"

"No. They said they'd put the word out to their patrol officers. They should be able to access records to get the make

and model of her car and plate number, but if she drove off
and got lost or forgot she was here to watch Jalen . . ."

"Does she have dementia?" That could explain things.

"Not that I know of."

Last night, Linc clarified that Regina wasn't *his* grandmother. This morning, Kendra dug through Bri's file. Somehow, she'd missed the note that her *paternal* grandmother took
custody of her after her parents were killed in a car accident.
However, Linc had been placed in foster care. She didn't need
to ask Linc about his relationship with Regina—they didn't
have one.

What kind of woman was Regina that she would split
them up? Linc wasn't her biological grandchild, but he and
Bri were half-siblings. Even without meeting Regina, Kendra
guessed that it had to do with Linc being bi-racial, while Bri
was Caucasian. And if that was the case, did it play into
Regina not showing up to get Jalen?

Being mixed-race, Kendra had experienced similar prejudices over the years, though not as much as her parents had
growing up when being bi-racial was less common. Doing the
work she did, Kendra had seen attitudes shift. Most people
had become more accepting, but prejudices didn't die
overnight.

"My in-law is a detective. I'll call Clara and see if she can
escalate the search," Kendra said.

"Appreciate it. I'm going by the dealership to see if any of
Bri's co-workers know where she was going and with who.
She had to have talked to someone."

"Do you know her friends here?"

Linc ran a hand over the back of his head. His impressive
bicep flexed as he shook his head. "No. Between work, her
Narcotics Anonymous meetings, and Jalen, she hasn't had
time to connect with a lot of people or get out. I told her when

I'm not deployed, I'd watch Jalen one night a week so she could take a class or find an activity to make friends, but we had a difference of opinion on that."

"What do you mean?"

"She wanted to take a painting class, and I suggested she take a continuing education class to increase her job marketability. She accused me of being a controlling dictator."

"You military types can come across as controlling."

"I was just trying to help. She's got an independent streak."

Kendra flexed her toes and kept her mouth closed rather than point out Linc was a typical male with his I'll-tell-you-how-to-solve-your-problems manner when Bri hadn't asked for him to run her life. "I'm sure she appreciates the help with Jalen. Being a single parent is hard, but she's working hard, making good choices, and being a great mom. She'll be devastated to know her Mrs. Feldman failed to pick Jalen up, and I was notified to get him. It's good you were coming back in time to intervene."

Linc diverted his gaze, and his mouth pursed.

In her line of work, she'd learned to read body language. "What are you not telling me?" After several seconds, he met her gaze.

"She left me a voicemail two days ago that she'd done something stupid. Before she could give details, someone came in, and she ended the call."

"Why didn't you say this last night?" This changed everything.

"I wasn't going to say anything in front of Jalen when I have no idea whether she'd had a car accident, forgotten to pay rent, or—" he sighed. "Or relapsed. When I couldn't reach her, I took emergency leave. That's why I'm here."

"If you'd told me—"

"It's not her fault her grandmother's gone MIA. The woman was hardly the best parent. Her son not only used but dealt drugs, and she let Bri go down the same damn path after she took her in. If I told you, you might put Jalen in foster care. And that is *not* happening."

He had a point about Regina, but Kendra didn't divulge the confidences that Bri had shared, which explained her self-destructive behavior. Trauma therapy had helped get her on the right path to recovery, but addiction wasn't an easy fix even when kids were around as motivation to stay clean. "How long is your leave?"

"As long as I need to be here for him."

"Are you on her account to track her phone?"

"No. She's still on the government assistance plan."

"I think it's best to let Clara know about the call. Maybe they can locate where Bri called from or trace her phone and find a way to contact her to let her know about Regina. Or do you think Regina went to help Bri and . . .?"

"I don't know what to think. I'm hoping like hell that they aren't connected and that Bri isn't in Mexico. Regina wouldn't have left Jalen to go to Mexico."

"I hope not." Kendra had been to Cancun with her ex-boyfriend, Marcus, two years ago. She'd felt safe at the beautiful resort. However, she was well aware of the problems with drug trafficking and stories of tourists being kidnapped for ransom. She didn't want to think of anything like that happening to Bri. "Here's the form for the drug test with instructions for them to send me the results."

He took the paper from her with a slight grumble. "I'll go get this knocked out and let you know if I learn anything at the dealership."

FIVE

It hadn't taken as long as he expected to get in for the drug test. From there, Linc went by the dealership and talked to several other service department employees. The males knew little about Bri other than that her clients loved her, and the female customers trusted her not to take advantage of them.

The receptionist was another younger female who sometimes ate lunch with Bri. She confirmed that Bri had gone to Acapulco, Mexico but she didn't know the name of the resort or friend she'd gone with. Bri had told her co-worker that this friend had booked an all-inclusive trip with her boyfriend, but after the pair split, she invited Bri to go rather than lose the non-refundable booking.

He could understand Bri not telling him about the trip. It's not like he was her keeper or father—as she often reminded him. Who was this friend, and was her plan to party in Mexico? He could think of a dozen stupid things Bri could be referring to, but were they related to Regina going MIA?

As he left the dealership, he decided to swing by his house to pick up clothes and continue to stay at Bri's apartment. While he didn't expect Regina to pop in like nothing had happened, it would be better for Jalen to be in his space with his bed, toys, and therapy items until this situation was sorted out.

Though Bri had gotten clean early in her pregnancy, Jalen had some mild developmental delays. Kendra had been instrumental in getting Jalen into OT and Speech therapy, and then intervention daycare. He admired Bri's dedication to doing various physical and speech exercises and working on her son's cognitive abilities. It wasn't easy, especially on her own, since whoever Jalen's father was, he wasn't in the picture. Unlike their mother, Bri had changed the trajectory of her life—for Jalen.

What's going on, Bri? If she'd call and let him know what she needed, he'd be there. This time, he'd save her.

After Bri had been arrested, he'd ignored Regina's mandate to stay out of his sister's life. Someone needed to keep her from flaming out, and Regina had lost control. He'd gotten Bri in a detox program, then brought her to Fayetteville from Atlanta. It'd taken a chunk out of his savings, but he hadn't regretted it with the turnaround she'd made.

He'd been with Regina several times for a holiday or Jalen's birthday parties. While she barely acknowledged Linc, he'd witnessed her accept and love her great-grandson—despite him looking nearly identical to Linc. Apparently, Jalen being *her blood* made a difference.

He needed to let it go. He'd survived. His experiences being in foster care toughened him. In the Army, he'd learned to protect himself and found a family forged by sweat, tears, and choice rather than blood. That didn't mean Bri and Jalen weren't his priorities, though.

His cell phone rang as he drove, and Kendra's name popped up on the display. If she already had the drug test results, she knew they were clean. "I just left the dealership, and it looks like Bri did go to Mexico."

"Clara just called. They found Regina's car."

A chill coursed through Linc. "Did they find her?"

"No. The car was in a grocery store lot overnight. The manager noticed it this morning and checked when they saw it was still there. They called it in when they saw a purse on the floor and found the car unlocked. Clara is on her way over. I thought you'd want to know."

"Do you have the address?"

"It was in Westwood shopping center."

"I'll head over there now."

"You don't need to do that. She'll update me."

"I can help." Despite his apathy for Regina, she was Bri and Jalen's relative and Linc needed to be there. He calculated a new route and turned at the next intersection.

"Just let the police do their investigation," Kendra continued.

"I did the drug test. Let me know if you need anything else." He tapped to end the call. Kendra had no idea what he did in the military And he refused to sit around doing nothing when his sister could be in trouble, and Jalen was affected.

Linc cruised into the lot and headed for the marked patrol car in the middle of an aisle behind a bright blue SUV with Georgia plates. He parked and headed over to where a redhead in a light blue button-down blouse and gray pants talked with a male patrol officer.

"Clara Andrews?" Linc asked.

The redhead turned and looked him over. "I'm Detective Clara *Lowe*."

"Lincoln Porter." He extended his hand. "I filed the report on Mrs. Feldman." He stepped closer to the car. "Did you find anything inside the vehicle?"

"Her purse was still inside with her phone and wallet, as well as groceries. We're going to have it towed for forensics to sweep. Do you know when Mrs. Feldman was last seen?"

"She dropped my nephew off at his school. That would have been around eight yesterday morning. She didn't show up to pick him up, so my guess is she was here before five."

"That'll help us narrow down the timeline. We'll get surveillance footage from the grocery and the surrounding stores in the strip mall to see if she left with someone or if the car was dumped here. That'll take a while."

"I can help review footage," Linc offered.

"Thank you, but we can handle this. At this point, there's no evidence of a crime—"

"Mrs. Feldman came to take care of my nephew. She doesn't know people here, so I don't see her going off with someone. I came home from deployment because I got a call from my sister indicating she might be in trouble. Now, I can't reach her, and she told her friends she was going to Mexico. I don't know if this is related, but it feels off." Way off. "I don't believe in coincidences. You can use me to help, but I won't be sitting on the sidelines waiting for you to find something."

Detective Lowe and the uniformed officer exchanged a brief look. "Are you in Third Group?"

"No."

She raised an eyebrow and studied him when he didn't say more.

"But I have US Marshal credentials," he added.

"All right. You can review footage to speed things along. *But* you can't go off on your own. You need to work *with* us."

"Acknowledged, ma'am." He didn't have to take orders from a civilian; however, he needed intel, and he couldn't get it through military channels. Without his team here, he was on his own, and he couldn't investigate like he needed *and* take care of Jalen.

SITTING in the police station less than an hour later, Linc reversed the footage from the grocery store's parking lot security camera that covered Regina's SUV. He stopped when he reached Regina parking. Zooming in, he confirmed that she exited the car and entered the grocery store—carrying the beige handbag found in the car.

Her purse being left in the car didn't sit right with Linc. Detective Lowe had already requested a warrant to access the call records and had gone in search of a charger that worked on Regina's ancient phone.

Watching for Regina to come out, Linc noted the vehicles in the lot and people entering the store. A nondescript white work van that had backed into a space down the aisle pulled out and took the handicapped parking spot next to Regina's vehicle as soon as the other sedan left.

Hair on his arms and neck stood at attention.

Linc decreased the speed of the playback. His pulse kicked up as he watched. The driver didn't get out of the van. From the security camera's angle, he could make out it was a dark-haired Caucasian or possibly Latino male wearing a ball cap pulled low and shielding his face.

When Linc saw Regina push a shopping cart into view, he shifted his focus on the man in time to see him climb into the back of the van. *Oh, shit.* He leaned closer to the screen and zoomed the image in on Regina, who loaded groceries into the back of her SUV. When she took the cart to the corral, the van's side door slid open. The man blocked Regina's path to the driver's side door.

Because the van's height obstructed the view below their heads, Linc couldn't tell from this footage how the man got Regina into the van so fast. In seconds, she was gone from sight. No one in the parking lot appeared to have witnessed what happened based on no one rushing forward to help.

The guy slammed the door closed and tossed Regina's purse in her car. Smart. No one could track her location via her cell if it wasn't on her. This guy knew what he was doing. They didn't have proof—yet—but this had to be tied to Bri's call.

He did his best to remain detached as he wrote down what he could see of the license plate when the van pulled out. Then, he watched which direction it took to determine what other cameras might give a better angle.

When Clara returned to her desk in the small squad room, he said, "I've got something."

She plugged the charger cord into the outlet built into her desk and stepped behind Linc. He backed up the footage and replayed it, fast-forwarding to the highlights.

She let out a sigh. "We need to review other angles, but I'm going with this as a kidnapping. I'll get a BOLO out on that van. Did you get the plate number?"

"A partial. Looks like they covered it with mud or something."

"Damn."

"Yeah. It's also the most common make and color, but there's a dent in the back bumper that could help identify it."

"Good catch." Clara picked up Regina's phone. "She's got message and voicemail notifications. I'll ask the judge to expedite the warrant on the phone."

"Or you can let me have a crack at unlocking it. You don't need a warrant when it belongs to the victim."

"Worth a shot, especially since it's already been nearly twenty-four hours." She handed Linc the phone.

He couldn't use biometrics unless he could get her prints from something at Bri's. Since it was a numbers pin code, he ruled out words. "What's her birthday?"

"You think it'll be that easy?" Clara opened Regina's wallet and read off the date.

"Nope." She'd never done anything to help Linc. He guessed she'd want something significant that she could remember. Next, he tried Bri's birthday, then Jalen's. Neither worked.

He tried to think like Regina. Clifton's birthday? He might have been a disappointment, but he'd been her son. More than once, Mom had done a combined birthday cake for Linc and Clifton since their birthdays were only six days apart. After trying Clifton's month, day, and year, he was locked out for the next minute.

"I'll check footage from the bank opposite the grocery. They've got better cameras. What's the time stamp on the van showing up?" Clara asked.

Linc gave her the time before trying the simple passcodes experts warned against using. He kept a list of the combos he tried. "Got it." Four-five-six-seven. At least it wasn't one-two-three-four.

He went to the text messages and opened the thread with Bri.

> The resort is gorgeous. Thanks so much for watching Jalen so I could come. Tell him I miss him already.

She'd attached two pictures. One was of the beach, taken from the deck of their room, and didn't include anything to identify the location. The other was a selfie of her blowing a kiss. He downloaded the images to Regina's phone and checked the details on the chance that, despite his warnings about protecting Jalen, she'd enabled location tagging. She hadn't. For once, he wished she'd bucked him.

Regina had three missed calls, all from a restricted number and in the space of about ten minutes yesterday afternoon. Possibly a debt collector or scammer. He hit the play button anyway. "It's Bri!" he alerted Clara and restarted the message.

"Grams, it's Bri." She spoke softly and urgently. "I'm calling from another number because Tonya—she isn't a friend—and I'm in trouble. She tried to trick me into smuggling drugs back into the States."

Linc's heart thumped against his ribcage. She wasn't using —but this could be worse. So much worse.

"I told her I won't do it. She's locked up my passport and claims the police here are on the cartel's payroll. I believe her. I don't know how I'll get out of here. She has pictures of Jalen outside his school and said she'd send her people there after him. I need you to pick him up *now*! Take him someplace safe. Don't go back to your house in Atlanta—"

"What are you—*you damn bitch*. Give me my phone."

It was the same voice as in the message Bri had left him. Angrier this time.

Based on the clank, the phone must have been knocked to the floor, and all he heard was grunts and banging.

Give her hell, Bri. Except Bri had never been a fighter.

"You're a sneaky bitch." Tonya's voice got louder. "Who were you calling? Your brother's deployed. He won't come running to help. Your Grams? Right," she taunted. "Hello. Hello? You just made things so much worse for yourself." The message ended.

Fuck. This had become the worst-case scenario. Except Tonya was wrong. Linc *had* come. And he'd find Bri.

He didn't have a number, and the phone was probably an untraceable burner. At least he had a name: Tonya. Whoever this woman was working with here had to be the one who took Regina. They hadn't gotten Jalen. The rock in Linc's gut grew to boulder size. "I need to get Jalen. *Now*."

"I'll send a patrol car to the school until you arrive," Clara offered.

"Good idea. See what you can find on that van," he requested then sprinted to the door.

He'd talked to Jalen's teacher this morning when he dropped him off to let her know he would be the one picking up Jalen. They wouldn't let anyone else take him, would they?

If Regina had answered or listened to the message, she would have taken precautions, though maybe they would have gotten Regina *and* Jalen.

What had they done to or with Regina? They might hurt her to motivate Bri to cooperate. Would they kill her? What were the chances they'd let her go?

Shit. How the hell would he protect Jalen and rescue Bri? With his team deployed, he was alone, with no idea where the hell in Mexico Bri even was.

SIX

That Linc had to buzz and wait to be let in the school made him feel better. However, he wasn't taking any chances leaving his nephew here or putting the other kids or employees in danger.

"Is everything all right with Jalen's grandmother?" the director asked as she escorted him to Jalen's room.

"Uh, I'm afraid she's still missing." He didn't elaborate.

"I'm sorry. Does you being here to get Jalen early have anything to do with the police cruiser out front?" Rachel paused outside the classroom.

He doubted much got by this woman. "It does. There's a possibility she may have been abducted."

"Oh, dear. At the risk of sounding paranoid, there was a white van parked in the elementary school lot next door last night."

Linc froze. "A minivan or . . ."

"No. A work-type van. It could have been a facilities maintenance van, but, while I was trying to get ahold of someone for Jalen, a man tried our front door. He didn't buzz but walked back toward the school and went off-camera. The van was the only vehicle there that late, and it left right after Ms. Andrews picked Jalen up. That he'd come to the door made me uneasy, but I didn't want to sound paranoid."

"No. You're right to be cautious. Did you get a look at the man?" Linc's training enabled him to project a calm demeanor as the director summoned the teacher and told Jalen to get his backpack.

"Mostly from behind. I think he was white, wearing jeans or dark pants, a gray shirt, and a black baseball cap. My guess is maybe five-foot-ten, average build, and late twenties or early thirties."

It sounded like the same man who'd taken Regina. If he'd followed Kendra last night, Linc needed to let her know as soon as possible.

"I get to leave early?" Jalen asked. "Is Mommy coming home?" His face lit up.

"Not yet, J-man. But we're going to have a little adventure." He hadn't thought beyond getting to Jalen, but these people knew where Bri lived. Tonya knew Bri had a brother. It wouldn't be hard to find out where he lived simply by checking property records. That complicated things.

ONCE KENDRA CONCLUDED her client interview, she checked her phone on her way to her car. Both the missed call and one of the text pings were from Linc. Before calling him back, she logged in to her email and verified his drug test results were clean. With that box checked off and him in charge of Jalen, she could focus on other things.

Linc answered before the second ring. "Have you talked to Clara?"

"Not since she called to say they had found Regina's car.

What did they find out?" Why hadn't she told Clara to call Linc directly? She'd done her job with Jalen, and it would be better for her to limit her interaction with Bri's brother, who stirred up too many complicated emotions. His dedication to Jalen and commitment to helping his sister were unexpected because of her Grandma Ruby's repeated warnings.

"The footage showed a man putting her into a van."

"Oh my goodness." Even with what Linc told her about Bri's call, she had not expected that.

"I need you to think..."

Linc's commanding tone didn't calm her.

"...when you picked up Jalen last night, did you notice a white van in the school lot next door that may have followed you?"

"Not then, but a white van?" Kendra's mouth went dry, and her breathing became labored.

"Yes. Why?"

"Because there was one parked next to me when I left the fast-food restaurant. The man sitting in the van had been eating near the play area, but he didn't have a child with him when he left." What if the man had tried to take Jalen? Thank goodness she'd sat right near the entrance to the play area and kept an eye on him while she'd made calls trying to arrange respite care. Had Regina been in that van?

"Did he follow you from there?"

She closed her eyes and thought back. "He turned out the same way I did. I was headed to the office, but when you called, I cut over to Bri's apartment. I don't remember seeing it after that. But Linc, I swear a white van followed me when I left my office this morning."

"Where are you now?"

"Leaving a client's home on the south side of town." Why would they still follow her? Studying the street, she didn't see a white van, but the man could have changed vehicles. "This was my last appointment of the day. I was headed back to my office, but someone needs to get Jalen."

"He's with me. Don't go to your office. Not with the possibility he was staking you out. Meet me at the police station. I'll fill you in there."

Good idea. Clara would know what to do. Kendra called her office to let them know she would be working from home the rest of the afternoon and drove to the police station gripping the steering wheel and checking her rearview mirror every few seconds.

KENDRA ENTERED the police station only a few minutes after Linc and Jalen had settled in to wait.

"Keep finding the matches while I talk with Ms. Andrews." He left Jalen doing one of his cognition exercises on the tablet and moved out of earshot to join Kendra at Clara's desk.

"We'll need your keys so they can sweep your vehicle just in case they put a tracker on it," Clara told Kendra, who handed her keys to a uniformed officer.

"What is going on? Do you think they'd track me?" Kendra cast a wide-eyed glance from Clara to Linc.

"It's possible." Clara filled her in on the phone message Bri had left for Regina.

Kendra sank into the chair next to Clara's desk. "This sounds bad."

His sister had done a great job conveying information about the situation, except for the vital piece Linc needed— where she was—so he could save her from being beaten, killed, or trafficked.

"These people don't mess around," Clara stated. "I'm not taking chances when it comes to you. Plates on the van were stolen, and we don't have a VIN number to know who it's registered to. Every patrol officer has been alerted to be on the lookout for it. I need the name of the restaurant you stopped at, what time you were there, and when you left. That could help us determine where he went last night. I also need the time you think you saw it outside the Social Services building, so we confirm if it was the same van you saw this morning."

"There's no guarantee he didn't follow her to Bri's place last night or home. You need to stay somewhere safe over the weekend until they catch this guy." Linc wasn't risking taking Jalen back to Bri's or even to his place.

"They may think Jalen is staying with you since you picked him up," Clara cautioned. "You need to stay with me and Derrick."

Kendra rolled her eyes. "They'll see I don't have him."

Clearly, she didn't understand the situation. "That doesn't matter. They may think that you know where to *find* him," Linc said. "These organizations can find out *who* you are and *where* you live. Who your family and friends are."

Kendra still didn't appear convinced.

"We had a mission that put my team in the crosshairs of a Colombian cartel. They couldn't find anything on us, as we keep low profiles, but they found out who the American pilot was who picked us up. They found her back here in the States. Even though we put protection protocols in place, they still got to her and took her to Colombia."

"Did they . . .?" Now Kendra's voice shook.

"We got her back. *Alive.* But it took our entire team. Our *highly elite* team." He let that sink in. "If they find you two are related, they *will not* care that you are a cop," he said to Clara. "You can't be around to provide twenty-four-seven security."

He shifted his focus to Kendra. "Do you have family or friends out of town you can stay with for a few days?"

"I'm not putting anyone I know in danger," Kendra stated.

She didn't leave him much of a choice. He wouldn't have to worry about her now that she'd been dragged into this, and she could watch Jalen while Linc did what he needed to do. "I've got a place. You and Jalen will be safe."

"Where?" Clara.

He hoped she'd agree and not buck his plan. "At one of my teammate's homes. He's deployed with me. Whoever these people are won't be able to connect us due to security protocols."

"We can't just break in and hide out at his house," Kendra protested.

"We wouldn't be breaking in. I have the code for the lock. With everything going on, you want me to call and ask permission?"

"Yes."

"She's a rule follower," Clara said, her lips tightening into a smirk.

He checked his watch. "My team's not gonna be happy if I wake them up."

Kendra crossed her arms.

He pulled his phone from his pocket and called Dev.

"Hey, man." Dev's low tone meant the team had turned in for the night. "Everything okay with Bri?"

"No. She was duped by someone to go on *vacation* in Mexico. The real purpose is to force her to smuggle drugs back."

"Shit. Did she know they were using her as a mule?"

"No. Somehow, she figured it out. They've got her passport and snatched her grandmother, who was watching Jalen."

"Shit," Dev said again. That was about the only swear word the Boy Scout used. "What are you gonna do?"

"Right now, I don't even know what city they went to. Police contacted the airlines, so I should have a destination and return flight info soon, but finding her Grams is our best shot at learning where they're staying so I can go down and bring her back."

Clara cleared her throat, and Linc angled away from her disapproving stare.

"On your own?"

Linc didn't like the doubt in Dev's voice. "What choice do I have?"

Dev's sigh weighed in across six time zones. "Let us know what we can do."

"We need a place to stay off their radar. Can we crash at your place?"

"You know you don't have to ask. Anything you and J-man need. Keys to the Camaro should be on the counter."

"You're fine with me borrowing your car?" he asked for Kendra's benefit.

"Not for teaching a defensive driving class, but other than that, yeah. Angela's been swinging by to start it up and takes the Ducati out every few weeks. I'll have Vincenti let her know you're there."

"Have him text me her number. I may need some intel she can access." With Angela's FBI and CIA background, Vincenti's girlfriend had connections that had helped the team in the past. Maybe she could pull a rabbit from the hat to find out who this Tonya was and where she and his sister were in Mexico.

"Just a thought," Dev used his diplomatic tone, "but her best shot could be to go with it. Bring the drugs in, then turn them over to authorities."

"But if she's caught, she could spend decades in a Mexican prison."

"She proves it was under duress. Testifies. She could get off. Better than what the cartel could do if she refuses."

"But there's no way to tell her that." They had her grandmother, but they knew she'd do anything to protect Jalen. They needed *him*.

SEVEN

After the tech confirmed there weren't trackers on their cars, Clara greenlit Linc's plan to have an officer drop Kendra's car at her apartment while they went to his friend's house. Kendra didn't get a say and couldn't even go by her apartment to get a change of clothes or a toothbrush. She was now going to be confined with her client's child—that part she was okay with—but also with Bri's alpha brother.

"I hungry." Jalen batted his long lashes at Linc as he buckled him in his booster seat.

"What do you want for dinner?"

"Hot dog with French fries and ketchup."

"Big surprise." Linc raised his gaze to Kendra. "Will's Grill okay with you? I doubt there's food at Dev's place."

"Sure." It beat fast food.

"We'll eat, and then you and I can build a fort in Mr. Devin's living room."

"Do I get to sleep in the fort?"

"You sure do."

"Can Champ come?"

"We left him at home, so not tonight. We'll bring him on our next camping trip," Linc promised.

"When's Mommy coming home?" Jalen asked.

"She's still on her trip," Linc said.

"Where's Grams?"

"She wasn't feeling well. But you've got me."

There was a definite catch in Linc's voice. Instead of his usual alpha warrior posture, he seemed like a regular human. One with vulnerabilities—at least when it came to kids. His patience in answering Jalen's barrage of questions made him attractive in a way Kendra had not counted on.

After they picked up their food, Linc drove to a neighborhood of mostly brick ranch homes close to the base. He got out and punched in the code on the keypad of the detached garage, then parked inside next to a sleek, red motorcycle. A sporty, metallic blue sedan occupied the right side of the garage.

The inside of his friend Devin's house was clean and decorated in a contemporary style. This guy liked nice things. It didn't jive with what she knew about Army salaries. She wondered what Linc's home looked like.

"You can have the main bedroom." Linc pointed to the open door before placing the bags of food on the kitchen table. He moved to the cabinet and removed plates.

"No need to dirty plates. We can eat out of the boxes," Kendra offered.

Linc's head jerked slightly, and the muscles in his back tightened. He turned and set the plates on the table. "We're worth it," he said tightly.

"I didn't mean—"

"It's okay," he cut her off.

Clearly, it wasn't. Dammit. He projected such confidence

that she hadn't anticipated his self-worth issues. But it was an issue common to former foster youth.

"What was the best thing you did at school today?" Linc waited until Jalen had taken a few bites to ask.

His little face scrunched up as he thought. "I did the obsacle course four times!" He held up four fingers.

Kendra smiled at the way he pronounced obstacle.

"Way to go, J-man. Did you pay attention during story time?"

Jalen gave an impish grin as his answer.

"Jalen," Linc warned.

"It was a loonng story." The kid drew the word out in a whine.

"Do you remember what the book was about?"

His mouth scrunched up, and he shook his head.

"You owe me a fry then." Linc reached for Jalen's French fries.

Jalen quickly pulled his plate close and covered it with his arms. "You have fries." He scowled.

"Yeah, but yours taste better." Linc held out one of his fries to Jalen, who dunked it in ketchup. "See?"

Jalen thoughtfully selected one fry and held it out. When Linc took a bite, Jalen laughed.

The way Linc engaged Jalen had Kendra's mind going places that would only end in disappointment—or worse. The realization that she was confined to this house with no real means of transportation made her chest tighten. She didn't have a choice. Even Clara agreed this was the safest option. She intentionally slowed her breathing. Linc wouldn't try anything, not with Jalen here.

In less than twenty-four hours, she'd gone from doing her usual thing as a social worker to being targeted by people associated with drug smugglers. That was insignificant compared to Jalen, who didn't know about either his mother or his grandmother. They'd taken him out of his familiar place and routine. Linc was here now, but what would happen with Jalen if something happened to Bri?

While she understood Linc wanted to help Bri, she needed to talk him out of his crazy ass plan to go to Mexico on his own. Even if Clara was right and he was in Delta—which was impressive—he needed to leave this to the proper authorities. Once Jalen was in bed, she could launch her battle plan.

Before she could clear their plates after they ate, Linc collected them and carried them to the sink.

"I'll do the dishes," Kendra offered.

"I got it. I said we'd use them. Besides, you're being inconvenienced already."

Jalen came to Linc's side with the hand towel as he rinsed the plates. "I help."

Despite turning her down, Linc handed him one.

"I can help around the house," Jalen sang.

"Good job, J-man."

"If I help Mommy, I get to watch a show. Can I watch *Bluey*?"

"We'll see if we can find it on the T.V. After we build the fort."

"Yay." Jalen nearly dropped the second plate.

While she imagined Linc's friend would love coming home to find preschooler shows on his recently viewed list, all Linc was doing with Jalen upped his relatability and appeal.

After finishing the dishes, Linc raided Dev's linen closet for spare sheets and blankets. When he carried out the sawhorses, she did a double take.

"Where did those come from?"

"The second bedroom. I was helping him with some renovations before we deployed."

She pulled out her laptop while he set up the sawhorses. He brought over two of the kitchen chairs, then draped a blanket over one side and anchored it with some books from the shelves on either side of the wall-mounted television. After he finished covering it, they had a fort far better than the blanket draped over two card tables she and her sister and cousins used to make.

He put a folded blanket down on the floor and added some pillows before Jalen crawled in.

"Come in, Uncle Linc," he pleaded.

Linc got on his hands and knees and crawled in.

Kendra's body temperature rose, and her ovaries came dangerously close to exploding. With his incredibly good looks, charming smile, muscular body and arms, intelligence, and love for kids, how was this man still single?

She shook her head as if that could dispel the thoughts going through her brain. Linc Porter was military and *not* the man for her. For all she knew, he might have a girlfriend. Not that she was going to ask. This arrangement was just for a day or two, then she'd resume her regular life, and he'd return to his.

As much as she detested the initial online matching process, once she was no longer a possible target of a drug cartel, it would be time to start thinking about dating again. She loved helping others but wanted her own family—a husband and kids.

Marcus hadn't been the right one—even though it broke her family's heart. But Prince Charming wasn't going to randomly knock on her door. She had to put herself out there.

EIGHT

Hunched over in the blanket fort, Linc used the T.V. remote to scroll through the streaming options to find a show for Jalen. He hadn't thought through bringing Kendra here with them. They didn't have a change of clothes or toothbrushes. Maybe he could rustle up something to make Kendra more comfortable. Dev had dozens of books she could pick from, ranging from biographies, history, action, mysteries, and spy novels, if she wanted to read. The guy was always reading during his downtime on deployments, unless there was a game going. None of the team played poker with him anymore—at least not for money.

Jalen stretched out on his stomach absorbed from the moment the show started.

Before they reached the opening credits, Linc's phone rang. Clara.

"I need to get this." Linc made his escape, awkwardly climbing over Jalen, who didn't budge.

"Did you find the van?" He settled on one of the chairs at the kitchen table.

"Do you have any idea how many white work vans are

registered in Cumberland County? The partial plate came back as a match to a similar make, but the plate was stolen the other night. And I wouldn't put it past them to steal another plate to make it harder to identify."

"You're right about that."

"I know. They're running the plates on every one patrol sees. They're looking for the dent in the back right bumper you noticed. But I do have good news."

Linc's heart rate kicked up.

"We found a flight reservation in Brianne's name. The seat next to her was for a Tawnya Fahey, spelled T-A-W-N-Y-A. Do you know her?"

"No. Where did they fly to?"

"Her last known address was in Atlanta. She's not living there anymore. We don't have a local address for her. No criminal records either. We're trying to get her credit card records to see if we can locate a hotel reservation."

"Where did the flight go?" he pressed after she ignored him the first time.

"Acapulco, this past Tuesday. We don't have the resources to call all the hotels and rental condos in Acapulco."

"Bri told her coworker it was an all-inclusive resort. That should narrow things down," Linc suggested.

"We can start there, but don't bank on that being true. Acapulco is typically safe, especially near the beaches. However, they grow poppies in the surrounding area, so you have major drug production. The government broke up the biggest syndicate, but now you've got smaller groups constantly fighting for control, and the region has some of Mexico's highest crime rates."

Clara wasn't telling Linc anything he didn't already know. Drugs, guns, human trafficking.

"The cartels are always looking for new ways to smuggle

drugs in. Most couriers get caught because they know they're carrying and act nervous. But, if they can get someone to transport it without their knowledge, they have a better shot of getting through security. They busted some guy in Charlotte a few weeks ago, coming back from a trip to Acapulco with his new girlfriend. Dogs alerted to his checked bag and found several kilos of cocaine in hidden compartments of his carry-on. He claimed the girlfriend had traded suitcases with him to bring back souvenirs and needed his bigger suitcase—and the trip was all her idea. Considering she disappeared after they pulled him in for an interview, they believe he was duped. It sounds like what could have happened with Bri."

Bri wouldn't have trusted a man wanting to take her on vacation, but a woman? Linc wanted to get his hands on this Tawnya. "When's the return flight?"

"This Tuesday."

That gave him a few days to get down there and find her. "You'll let me know if you find out where they're staying?"

"You are not going to Mexico."

"It's not like *you* can," he countered.

"Not me personally, but federal agencies and agents will work with locals there to find your sister. Involvement by US military personnel is prohibited and could have serious political ramifications."

He wouldn't be going in a military capacity. He was officially on leave.

"We're still reviewing footage to determine where the van came from or where it went after they took Mrs. Feldman. Right now, she is our priority. Other than the phone call you got from your sister, there's no evidence of foul play regarding Bri. We're trying to get Mexican authorities to provide the location of the last cell tower Bri's phone connected with. We also have an alert set up if her phone turns on to try to trace it."

Linc didn't put much stock in that happening. If Bri called from Tawnya's phone, it meant she couldn't access hers. He'd bet money it had been destroyed. "What about Bri's text messages and call log? Have you gotten anything from her provider?"

"They wouldn't release anything without a court order, and it's Friday—"

"Are you saying you're not going to get anything until Monday?"

"That's a possibility unless we can find Mrs. Feldman and prove there was a crime. I'm leaving the office; however, I'll be digging into this Tawnya woman, looking for anything that might help. You take care of Jalen and Kendra and let the police do our job."

"Acknowledged, ma'am."

"Which you said before and isn't the same as agreeing."

"If you find Mrs. Feldman or anything else on Tawnya, let me know." He ended the call. If she thought he was going to sit around on his ass while his sister was in danger, she did not understand the mindset of a Special Forces operator. No one was more trained than him to get his sister back.

NINE

After Linc ended the call with Clara, he disappeared into the main bedroom. Kendra debated with herself before following him.

"What are you doing?" she asked when she found him rummaging through a vanity drawer. An empty shoe box and a small black hard-shell case with a combination lock sat on the counter.

"Looking to see if Dev has any spare toothbrushes."

"What's in that case?"

Linc hesitated and pushed the case further from her. "Dev's personal weapon. It might not be safe to go to my house to get mine since I can't rule out Tawnya having more than the one accomplice who snatched Regina. I'm not taking any chances with Jalen or you."

"Either keep it locked up or unloaded with Jalen in the house. Kids his age don't understand the danger."

"I know that."

She shrank back at his tone. "I am not your enemy, Linc." And it was going to make being together harder if they treated each other like adversaries. "We both want the same thing—

Bri home safely and what's best for Jalen. Maybe we should address the elephant in the room."

"What's that?" He put the top on the shoe box and placed it on the highest shelf in the closet.

He was going to act like it hadn't happened or didn't mean anything? Or maybe he had an ulterior motive in trying to help Bri back then too. "That you asked me out, and I had to turn you down."

"That was a long time ago, and whatever. You had your reasons." He picked up the gun case and started to move past her.

"Whatever?" She didn't expect him to be mooning over her, but they needed to get along while they were stuck together.

He raised an eyebrow. "I understood the girls in high school not wanting to go out with me when I was a foster kid, but that's my past. I turned out all right. I thought you'd be the last person to—"

"You think *that's* why I turned you down?"

He shrugged.

He had nerve calling her character into question and thinking she'd be that shallow when he knew nothing about her. "That had nothing to do with it. I didn't even see that in Bri's file."

"You're going to stick to the conflict of interest because I'm your client's brother, then?"

"It *was* a conflict of interest." That should have been reason enough, so she hadn't explained the entire reason then, but now? Maybe if he understood her family background, it would make this easier. "The women in my family have a bad history when it comes to military men."

"You said no because I'm in the Army? What? You're saying you've sworn off *all* military men?"

"If I don't want to be disowned by my family. Particularly my Grandma Ruby."

"That seems a little extreme. Did she get dumped or cheated on more than once?"

"She got pregnant and then abandoned."

"Okay. But because one guy's an ass—"

"There's more. When my mom was a toddler, Grandma Ruby met a great guy, also a soldier. They married before Vernon left for his second tour in Vietnam, and she got pregnant right away. They wanted to have a child together in case anything happened to him. Which it did."

"He was killed in action?" Linc's tone dropped a level.

"Four months into his deployment. But she had to keep going for her girls."

"That's not his fault."

"No, but she'd been abandoned and widowed, then came strike three—this time a Vietnam veteran who was out of the military. They started dating, and he moved in, but she wouldn't marry him because then she would lose her survivor benefits."

"Smart move on her part."

"Definitely. They didn't talk about PTSD much back then. Instead of treatment, he self-medicated with alcohol and became abusive. Verbally, then physically. After she kicked him out, she swore off military men and forbade her daughters from getting involved with any as well."

"Yet she stayed in Fayetteville? Home of the largest Army base."

"This was her home, and she had family here," Kendra explained. "My mother was always a rule follower, so she didn't date any that she admitted to. However, my aunt probably had a romanticized view of the military since her father, Vernon, was the love of Ruby's life. Despite Grandma's warnings, my aunt dated soldiers, and they fought about it until my aunt moved out. She married a soldier, and they had two sons. Things got ugly because he cheated on her. One night, they got into a fight. She locked herself in the bedroom, got his gun, and when he broke through the door, she shot him." Kendra rarely shared this story, yet here she was, standing in some stranger's bathroom telling Linc, hoping he'd understand without her having to tell him more.

"Did he survive?"

"No." Because she'd let him bleed out rather than call 9-1-1. "My aunt was sentenced to five years for voluntary manslaughter. My parents took in my cousins, and Grandma Ruby moved in to help take care of all four of us preteens. She still lives with my parents. Lamont and Derrick—Clara's husband—lived with us for five years, so they're more like brothers than cousins."

"I get the family history, but you're stereotyping all military men. There are bad players in any profession. Most of the men I work with exemplify integrity and honor." He paused, holding eye contact with her. "Have you had any personal experience to justify your blanket exclusion?" His eyes narrowed more, and his expression and tone softened.

The pressure in her chest expanded. "I have." However, she was not sharing details. "It didn't end well." She'd thought Don was an honorable guy—until the night of their third date. She'd already learned her lesson when Linc asked her out months later. She'd followed Grandma Ruby's advice rather than give in to the temptation of her client's sexy and protective brother. And she put Linc out of her mind—until yesterday. "Now you know, it's nothing personal or about your history. It's strictly *my* history and *my* issues."

"I'm sorry you felt I was treating you like an enemy. That was not my intent. You've been good to Bri and Jalen. I'm worried about Bri—and Regina—and feel helpless." He swallowed and let out a heavy breath.

"Trust that Clara and the police are doing everything they can." She laid a hand on his arm, then removed it once she realized what she'd done. "You need to be here for Jalen."

"Yeah. I need to get back out there." He hesitated. "Thanks for explaining. Though I still think you're wrong for stereotyping all of us military guys."

At least he cracked a smile.

Linc stowed the gun case on top of the fridge. "After this episode, it's bedtime, J-man. I need to hit the rack too." Linc pulled out another sheet from the linen closet and covered the couch.

"You're not going to sleep in the other bedroom?" This guy really would do anything for his nephew.

"We hadn't finished the renovations before we left. There's no bed."

He'd known that when he picked this as their safe house. What did that mean? "You two should take the main bedroom. I can sleep on the couch."

"We're good. He's got the fort, and a couch is a step up from the Army bunk I've been sleeping on."

"All right." She picked up her computer bag and purse. No point in fighting him on this.

"Let me find you something more comfortable to sleep in." He headed back into Dev's bedroom.

"It's okay. We're invading his space already."

Despite her protests, Linc opened the dresser drawers and pulled out a T-shirt and a pair of gym shorts. "He won't mind," he promised, laying them on the bed. "See you in the morning." He closed the bedroom door behind him.

In the otherwise silent house, Kendra made out Jalen asking to call his mom to say good night, then left an excited message telling Bri about making a tent and how he would sleep in it. He added that he missed her and wanted to hug her soon.

Kendra sniffed back tears. I would be so hard for Jalen if Bri went to prison or worse.

"Go to the bathroom. Then I'll read you a story," Linc said.

"I don't have my jammies."

"You don't need them tonight. Bri," Linc's voice got louder, like he'd moved closer to the primary bedroom to keep Jalen from overhearing. "We got your message to Regina. Jalen's with me, and I won't let anything happen to him. If you get this, do whatever you have to do to get back here."

TEN

Linc managed to catch a full seven hours of sleep before jolting awake at dawn. With Jalen still sound asleep, Linc checked his phone to see if there was a message or text from Bri or the police about finding Regina.

The only text was a response from Dev with the combination to his gun case.

Rather than wake Kendra, he texted to let her know he was going out for provisions and asked her morning beverage preference in case she preferred fancy coffee drinks. With Dev's loaded Sig Sauer strapped on, Linc grabbed Dev's keys and slipped quietly out of the house.

He'd nearly finished in the grocery store when his phone chimed. *I don't deserve it, but I need a miracle.*

It was just Kendra replying instead of Bri or Clara. He backtracked and picked up a box of English Breakfast tea. Good thing he asked. So far, he'd been off on everything he thought about Kendra.

He'd been wrong about her reason for rejecting him, but that she didn't date military guys made it a moot point. That's who he was. The military had been his best option when he aged out of foster care. It provided financially and had given him skills and access to higher education that had otherwise been out of his reach. He had twelve years of service behind him and planned to do at least another eight to hit twenty and full retirement. He'd likely stay in longer. His team was his chosen family, and he wasn't giving up on them or his career because of a woman, especially since marriage was not in his plans. Not with his past. It's one reason he'd pursued the dangerous path of Special Forces. He wouldn't have to worry about leaving a wife or kids to manage on their own if something happened to him. Not the way he and Bri had been left behind.

That Kendra didn't give details on what happened with the military guy she dated, despite disclosing everything else, had kept him awake last night. But he hadn't asked. She'd gotten stuck in this situation and was helping him out. No point in pressuring her when there was a lot of family history there already. Too much to overcome. He'd learned you couldn't make people change their prejudices, and it wasn't worth trying. Better to let it go and not let them hurt you more.

"Your Uncle Linc's back," Kendra said when the garage door went up. She couldn't blame the boy for being anxious after he woke up to find Linc gone. She'd panicked that he'd taken off for Mexico and left her here with Jalen until she saw the text he'd sent. Hopefully, he'd accepted the futility of trying to rescue Bri on his own, though she doubted he gave up easily.

"Help me with these groceries, J-man." Linc entered carrying several bags.

"Did you get me chocolate milk?"

"Of course. I'm your favorite uncle for a reason."

Jalen gave him an adoring smile, and Linc smiled right back. "And Captain Crunch?"

"Yes, since it's the weekend." Linc handed two of the bags to Jalen, and they carried them into the kitchen. Then, he went out and retrieved another load.

"How long are you thinking we're going to be here?" Kendra eyed the covered island. She'd thought this would be a day or two at most. She had a job and a life—*and* he probably thought he was doing his by keeping her safe.

"I don't know. Hopefully, this is overkill. I can always take the food to Bri's, but if I go down to Mexico, I want you and Jalen to have what you need so you don't have to go out."

And poof went her hopes they could avoid another difficult conversation.

"Can you open dis?" Jalen handed her the cereal box.

"Sure."

Jalen went around the island and climbed onto the bar stool.

Linc loaded groceries in the fridge and avoided her gaze as she poured Jalen a bowl of cereal.

"Have you heard anything from Clara or the police?" she asked when he handed her the box of tea.

"Not yet. Dev must have filled in Chief Lundgren because I got a text from his wife, Stephanie. She's the head of the Family Readiness Group and reached out to the other wives. They've offered to help watch Jalen. I wasn't sure about it, but no one would know to find Jalen with them, and Walt Shuler didn't deploy because he's transitioning to a different role. He's around, there's good protection, and they have a couple of kids Jalen can play with today. That frees me up to search for the van. You can stay here or come with me."

"What are you going to do if *you* find the van?"

Linc hesitated. "That depends."

"On . . .?"

"On where it is and what intel I can get."

"Then I'm coming with you." She could call Clara and insist he let the police handle it if, by some miracle, they did find the van. Staying in a stranger's home alone not knowing if Linc was doing something reckless would stress her out all day.

As they drove to his friend's house, Linc told Jalen they were taking him to play with Mr. Walt's kids and have lunch while he and Kendra worked.

"Can we go to that playground?" Jalen asked as they drove past an elaborate climbing structure with tubes and slides.

"I'll tell Mr. Walt you want to go." Linc parked on the street in front of his teammate's house. "Do you want to come in and meet the Shulers?"

"Okay, but I do trust your judgment." They'd also had to pass through security to get on base, which would make it harder for whoever had taken Regina to get to Jalen if they found out where he was.

Linc unbuckled Jalen and carried the booster seat with him to the door.

A woman in her late thirties opened the door, still wearing her pajamas. "Come on in."

"This is Jalen," he introduced them as Jalen hugged Linc's leg.

"I'm Miss Tammy." Behind her, two kids popped into view and stared at Jalen. The younger girl followed her brother to their mother's side. "This is Beckham and Emma."

"Do you want to play with my truck?" Beckham held a yellow toy dump truck.

"Can I?" Jalen looked at Linc.

"Give me a hug first." Linc dropped to a knee. His eyes closed as Jalen wrapped his arms around his neck, and he hugged the boy back.

"You're squeezing me," Jalen croaked dramatically.

"Sorry," Linc chuckled. "Have fun and play nice. I'll see you tonight." Moisture glistened in his eyes as he got to his feet. As Walt joined them, the boys scurried into the adjacent room, followed by the young girl. "You're sure this isn't an imposition?"

"Not at all," Tammy assured him. "It'll keep those two from tormenting each other."

Walt nodded his agreement as he shook hands with Linc. "Sorry to hear about your sister."

"Thanks. This is Kendra Andrews. She knows Bri. We're trying to locate the van that snatched Bri's grandmother. If we can find her, it could give us a lead on where Bri is."

"If there's anything I can do, or you need backup, let me know."

"For now, keep him safe." Linc nodded to where the kids had disappeared.

"I got your six. How's the new guy doing? He earned his nickname yet?" Walt asked.

"He's still Newbie, and not happy about it."

Tammy rolled her eyes. "Team tradition," she explained to Kendra. "You should let the wives contribute ideas."

"Not happening. I can't have all the guys calling me McSteamy or Mr. Buns of Steel," Walt cracked.

Tammy laughed out loud and patted his backside. "In your dreams."

Kendra eyed Linc. "And yours is?" Why did she desperately want to know his nickname?

"It's classified."

Based on his grin, that wasn't true, though that beat his usual intense expression. When he aimed his smile at her, it had an even more disarming effect than when he smiled at Jalen.

"If he gets wound up, swinging or having him go in circles helps ground him," Linc shared. "There's a change of clothes in the backpack, just in case. If you tire him out at the playground, he might take a nap for you. Call me if you need anything."

ELEVEN

"Did you want to check in with Clara for any updates?" Kendra asked him as they left the Shuler's.

"I figured she'll call if she learns anything she can share," he deflected.

Based on her clearing her throat, she disapproved. Part of him wished she'd stayed back at Dev's. Having her along complicated things. If they did find the van, he couldn't risk her safety, and she'd want to report the findings to the police. But she was here, and having a second pair of eyes wouldn't hurt when they had so much ground to cover.

He'd tried thinking like a drug-smuggling kidnapper and ruled out anywhere with a high-density population, where neighbors could see or overhear. If these guys were connected to some higher-level players, they could even be in an upscale neighborhood with the van parked in the garage, making it harder to find. The low odds of this mission's success weighed on him, but he had to try.

As he drove to the first neighborhood he planned to scout, his phone rang. Clara's name on the display gave him goosebumps.

"Did you contact her?" he asked Kendra before answering.

"Not since yesterday."

Let this be good news. "Did you find Mrs. Feldman?" he asked.

"Good morning to you too. No, we have not. However, from reviewing video footage, we determined the van came from South McPherson Church and headed back that way after taking her. We lost them after crossing Cliffdale. We're concentrating our search in that quadrant."

"Good to know." He was on the right track.

"What are you doing?" When he didn't answer, she continued. "I can tell you're in the car."

"Performing a grid search."

"You left Jalen and Kendra at your friend's?"

"No," Kendra piped up. "He left Jalen with a teammate's family, and I'm helping."

"Oh, jeez," Clara groaned.

"I've got nothing else to do," Linc said. "And no one would know the car we're in. It's less likely to alert the kidnapper than police cruisers." That he could have ditched the van by now wasn't outside the realm of possibility, but he had to keep looking.

She sighed. "I can't stop you, but if you find anything, you need to report in and let us handle it."

"Acknowledged."

"Stop giving me that 'acknowledged' bullshit. I want you to agree." For someone half Chief Lundgren size, her authoritative tone sounded a lot like his superior.

"Yes, ma'am. If we find the van, we will contact authorities." Kendra wouldn't give him a choice. "Any reports on more stolen license plates?"

"No, though, if it were me, I'd get a plate that wouldn't be missed right away. Like from a car in a long-term parking lot."

"Exactly." For being a small-town detective, she impressed him. But he couldn't leave it all to them. Not when this was Bri. He couldn't let her down—again.

For the next three hours, he drove down every street in several residential neighborhoods, ruled out all three white work vans they'd seen, and had hardly put a dent in the search area. Man, he wished the team were here to help. Kendra kept a list of streets, which helped when things began to run together. "Let's take a break and get some lunch," he suggested.

"Did you want to go to the drive-thru someplace?"

"It should be fine going in to eat. Is Panera okay?"

"Perfect. I never get tired of eating there."

For once, he'd guessed right. They ordered at the counter and got their beverages. When he placed his hand on her arm to steer her away from a table in the center of the room, she flinched and pulled her arm away.

"Sorry. I was just going to say let's sit there." He pointed to a vacant booth in the back of the dining room.

"It's okay." She licked her lips.

No, it wasn't okay. A person didn't react that way to an innocent touch without a reason. Bri was proof of that.

He took a seat facing Kendra's appealing face and the restaurant's interior. Despite the astronomically remote chance of Regina's abductor walking in, Linc's gaze swept over the diners and to the door with each new arrival as they waited for their food. "I'm sorry you got dragged into this."

"It's not your fault. You had no way of knowing. None of us did. It's Bri and Regina that I'm worried about. And Jalen," she added.

"Level with me. If something happens and Bri doesn't

make it back here, what are my chances of being given custody?"

"I can't say for certain. There's an excellent chance if she named you as custodian in a legal document. I know you have to have a family care plan for deployments, but Jalen's going to have to continue in therapy for a few years. If Regina is found, at her age, it's not likely she can provide the level of care he needs. If you don't have other family as backup, you'd have to consider who could handle that kind of commitment. That can be a lot for someone to take on. It isn't ideal for Jalen to be placed with a family he doesn't know either," she cautioned. "If you were in a position that didn't deploy or got out of the military, that would change things."

"What other options are there?" He hated to ask.

"He could go into foster care. He's young. There are families he could be placed with who are looking to adopt. Just this week, I met with a couple—"

"No. I wouldn't have a say on who. They may not allow me to stay a part of his life. Or they could move. Jalen might think I'd abandoned him." That he wasn't worth sticking around for.

"You could ask someone you know to adopt him."

Except Linc didn't know who he could ask. That left him one option: get Bri home safely. If he failed, it might be the end of his time on the Bad Karma team or in the Army.

Half an hour after they had resumed their search, Kendra sighed and angled to face him in the car. "So, after your mother died in the car accident, Bri went to live with her grandmother, but you went into foster care?"

"Yep." Memories of Regina driving away with Bri resurrected that sick to his stomach, helpless feeling. "Bri and I wanted to stay together; however, our social worker said it would be difficult to place us together."

"And Mrs. Feldman wouldn't take you?"

"I wasn't her blood. She was certain I'd be a bad influence. Steal or get involved in drugs because I was a Black teenager. Never mind that was her white son's MO, and she let Bri go down that same path as her son and our mom." But for different reasons.

"Yet, we're out here looking for her." Kendra scanned the cars on her side of the street.

"I'm doing it for Bri. And for Jalen."

"I'm guessing foster care wasn't the best experience."

"It wasn't that much worse than home. At least there was food. They encouraged me to do my schoolwork. I only got roughed up by the older boys in the first of the three group homes I was placed in." He didn't expect someone to adopt him, but there'd been no love. No feeling like he had worth. He couldn't put Jalen in a situation like that.

"The other kids beat you up?"

"I was smaller than them, and I wasn't black enough for my foster brothers." Just like he wasn't white enough for Regina. His Bad Karma teammates didn't care about his skin color. "You probably understand what it's like. People asking *what you are*. You're multiracial is my guess." And beautifully so.

"I do get asked that a lot. Usually, it's curiosity since people like to put you in a category. Black, White, and Korean mix is not all that common." She smiled as she said it. "Both my parents are bi-racial, so I'm second generation, and they helped navigate the uncomfortable questions and prejudices they knew would come up."

"That would have been helpful." He didn't mean to say

that out loud. "Bri saw some of it with me as her brother, but seeing it isn't the same as experiencing it."

"People have different experiences being mixed-race. You being raised by your white mother with your white sibling was different than my father being a Black Asian raised by a middle-class white family—"

"What?"

"He was adopted."

"I guessed that much. But it's still unusual."

"My grandfather was a doctor and went on several medical mission trips. When he went to Korea, my grandmother decided to join him, and they brought their son, my Uncle Matt. They worked at orphanages where kids don't get the medical care they need. There were a lot of kids fathered by American service members during and after the Korean War. Korean culture is big on family lineage and, unfortunately, rarely adopt, especially mixed-race children. At that time, a Korean national was defined as any person born to a Korean *father*. So, if the father was of a foreign nationality, the child wasn't even considered a citizen. Most of those kids were sent to orphanages and institutions."

"I never heard that about the citizenship," Linc said.

"Not many people have. It changed in the late nineties. Anyway, while my grandparents were at the orphanage, Uncle Matt played with the kids, and at the end of the second day, he said one toddler was going to be his brother."

That sounded like something Jalen would say. "How old was your uncle?"

"I think five. My grandparents thought it was cute but tried to explain they couldn't just take a baby home with them. As the week passed, he became even more adamant that this little boy was supposed to be his brother. My grandmother had miscarried twice, and she started to get on board with the idea, but my grandfather was not."

Linc wondered if that had to do with race.

"They hadn't even talked about adoption before this trip," Kendra continued as if reading his mind. "But my grandmother said she felt called to come with him this time, and maybe that little boy was why. Their story is that after a particularly long day working at the orphanage, my grandfather sat in one of the rocking chairs to take a quick nap and woke up with Dad sleeping on his chest."

"And that did it?"

"Pretty much. They talked to the staff about what they needed to do to adopt him that night. It took several months to make it happen, but any doubts that they were meant to make him part of the family were gone."

"Did his adoption play into you becoming a social worker?" he asked.

"A little. I think it was more that we took in Lamont and Derrick after what happened with my aunt. My background gave me a heart to advocate for kids and see things from a parent's perspective. We all mess up sometimes and need a second chance to prove our past doesn't define us."

"Like Bri. Having Jalen may have saved her life. She was scared, but he gave her a reason to do better. Though I had to convince her she could do it—if she got clean. She sure didn't have a good role model."

"Sometimes learning what behaviors we *don't* want to emulate is as beneficial as ones we do. And she truly participated in the parenting classes rather than just show up or expect somebody else to do all the work."

"Learning what resources were available to help with Jalen gave her confidence that she could do it and that she wasn't totally on her own. Then something like this happens." It was eating him from the inside out.

"Your sister's not their first target. I'm sure they've got the story down pat to reel people in."

"If she'd told me about the trip, I would have been suspicious. Then she wouldn't be in this jam."

"It's not your fault."

Maybe if he hadn't been overbearing out of fear that she'd backslide, she would have told him what was going on in her life. More than once, she'd told him to be her brother and to stop trying to be a father figure. Not that he knew how to be a father. Clifton had never been a real father, even after he and Mom had Bri. Mostly, he came around when he needed a place to stay or hoped to get laid. They could have used those parenting classes. Bri invited Linc to go with her to the class, but with his schedule and the fact he was never having kids, he hadn't made the effort. Why want something he couldn't have?

They drove down several streets in silence before they both spotted a white van simultaneously.

Kendra sat up straighter. "That looks like the one I remember."

The van backed into the drive and the shrubs' overgrown state were both indicators that this could be the one.

"I'll call Clara to send a patrol car to check it out," Kendra said as they cruised slowly past the house.

"No." He studied not only the house but the neighboring ones and continued down the block, ignoring Kendra, though fully aware of her staring and her phone in her hand. Even though a female would be less suspicious, he wouldn't ask *her* to approach the house with the potential kidnapper inside. "I'm going to go around the corner and get out. Wait until I get to the house to drive past and wait for me."

"You heard what Clara said."

"I'm only going to peek at the bumper and get the plate. It'll save the police time and resources if it's not the van. And, if it is and he sees a cop car, that could end badly for Regina."

"What if he sees *you*?"

"I'll roll with it."

Kendra shook her head. "I know you're armed, but this is not a plan."

He pulled the car to the curb and shifted it into park. "I'm asking you to trust me. I know what I'm doing." He put his hand on the door handle.

"I'm going to have 9-1-1 up and ready to connect."

"Only if there's an emergency."

"Like you get shot?"

"You don't have to wait for that. If you see a gun, call." He exited the car before she could call Clara. If no neighbors were outside, he could slip in and be back down on the street in less than ten seconds. He had this, and he needed a break.

He hadn't reached the driveway where the van was parked before a dog yapped from inside. Great. Once he passed the van, he detoured up the side for a quick look. Not seeing a dent in the bumper, he didn't bother recording the plate.

"What are you doing there?" An older woman's voice called out just before a barking tan and black ball of fur stopped a few feet away.

He calmly turned and reached for his wallet. "US Marshal, ma'am." He smiled and flipped his wallet open to his badge and credentials as a member of the elite Delta unit. "A similar van was used in an abduction."

The woman with gray-streaked hair and thick glasses scooped up the dog, which continued to bare its teeth. "My husband uses this van for his upholstery business. He ain't involved in no abduction."

"I already confirmed this wasn't the van used," he said as a slightly stooped man in his sixties exited the house. Definitely not the kidnapper in the video. "I'm sorry to have disturbed you, ma'am."

The woman watched him walk to Dev's car, which Kendra had stopped just past their driveway. "Hope you find 'em."

He gave a grim nod.

"Not the right van?" Kendra asked when he slid into the passenger seat.

He shook his head. "You didn't call the police, did you?"

"No. I didn't honk to warn you either when she came out." A bit of a smile played on her face as she drove.

"I wouldn't shoot an unarmed woman or yappy dog." He smiled back at her. The chill between them had thawed considerably since last night, and she was proving to be a good ally. And the most attractive one he'd worked with, but he needed to keep focused on his mission. It'd been over two days since Regina had been forced into the van. Was she still alive? Was Bri?

They drove around another four hours with no more scares and no success finding the van. "We should probably call it a day and get Jalen," he conceded.

"I'm guessing you'd prefer we not go by my apartment, but can we stop somewhere so I can buy a change of clothes if we'll be staying at your friend's house another night?"

"We can stop at the Post Exchange on base on the way." That would be safe.

They only spent about ten minutes picking up some clothing without bothering to try things on. After Kendra loaded her items at the checkout, Linc removed the divider she placed on the conveyor belt.

"I've got this." He inserted his credit card to pay as she discreetly bagged the pack of underwear she'd selected without him getting a good look. He couldn't help but picture her in a black lace bra and pair of hi-cut panties, even though that was not what she had bought. However, they weren't granny panties. That would have killed his little fantasy. For all he knew, she could be dating someone. It's not like he'd asked, though she also hadn't called anyone to cancel plans or give an update on her situation.

He waited until they got to the car to call the Shulers.

"I was just about to call you," Walt greeted him. "Any luck?"

"Afraid not. We're on our way to pick up Jalen."

"We're about to eat dinner, but the kids wanted to know if he could spend the night. They've been cooking up plans to turn the bunk beds into a tent."

"That's my fault. I made him a tent fort last night."

"It's all good. They've gotten along great. This way, you can keep doing what you need to do."

"Let me talk to him for a minute."

"Hello," Jalen didn't sound overly enthused to be interrupted to talk on the phone.

"I hear you're having a good time there, J-man."

"Uh-huh. Cans I spend the night, *please*?" He drew out the word.

"All right. If you need anything, have Mr. Walt call me." Linc held the phone further away as the boys squealed.

"Guess you said yes," Walt said.

"I did, but if he changes his mind in the middle of the night, just call me."

"I don't see that happening. I wore these kids out. We

spent two hours at the park, and I made them do PT and run drills. If he tells you I shot him, it was with a water pistol, and they both shot me back."

Linc laughed. "I appreciate you, man. See you tomorrow." He ended the call and started the car. "Guess we're free to keep searching for a bit. If you're done, I can always drop you back at the house."

She sighed lightly. "I'm good for a while longer."

"Dinner first, or resume our search?"

"Whatever you think is best." She looked out the car window.

"We'll eat and then cruise around. That way, it'll be dusk or dark in case I need to get up close with another vehicle." He tried to lighten the mood but didn't get a response. "I'd love some Chinese food."

"Sounds good."

What had he said or done wrong to warrant this sudden aloofness? Did she think Jalen was too young for a sleepover? He had memories of being left alone overnight with Bri when she wasn't much older. Maybe he should have asked Kendra before committing, but he wouldn't disappoint Jalen by changing his mind now.

After they ate, they canvassed neighborhoods until depleting the adrenaline and caffeine fueling him. "Let's call it a night." He'd catch a few hours of sleep and head out again.

TWELVE

Neither she nor Linc said much on the short drive back to Devin's house. Rising anxiety jumbled her thoughts even though she practiced her controlled breathing, and she tried to visualize and plan what she'd do once they arrived so she'd be in control.

After Linc parked, they retrieved the bags from the trunk. He unlocked the door and flicked on the lights inside. Setting the bags on the kitchen table, he turned to address her before she could escape to the bedroom. "Do you want to tell me what's wrong?"

"Nothing."

He gave a gruff semi-laugh and cleared his throat. "I'm not buying that. Do you think Jalen's too young to sleep over or that he's unsafe there? Because I—"

"I'm sure he's just as safe there or even more so. I wish you'd asked me before making the decision."

His mouth hung open before he said a soft, "Oh." He closed his eyes, and his lips disappeared as his head bobbed slightly. "With how you pulled away at lunch, I should have realized . . ."

"Realized what?"

"You're afraid to be here alone with me. Look, you can trust me," he continued when she didn't immediately deny it. "Do you know what happened to Bri?"

"She shared her history when I became her case worker so I could get her plugged into the right resources." His perceptiveness shocked her into answering. Bri might have shared more with her than Linc even knew about.

"I get it. And you should know I'm the last person who'll take advantage of you having to be holed up with me here. If there were another option to make sure you were safe and *felt* safe, I wouldn't make you stay here, but . . . You can lock the bedroom door," he offered lamely.

She nearly snorted at that. After he picked the lock to Bri's door in under a minute, she knew a bedroom door lock was in no way a deterrent. "I'll be all right. Please, don't take it personally. It's not you. It's the situation." And having lost all control, though, his addressing this let her breathe almost normally again.

"Can I ask a question?"

"Why not?" She braced herself for this to get even more uncomfortable.

"Does this have to do with the soldier you had a bad experience with?"

"It does," she admitted, since he'd probably know if she lied.

Linc's expression twisted. Veins on his arms popped as his hands clenched into fists. "The son of a bitch," he muttered. "I hope you reported him for rape, and his ass was kicked out of the Army."

"He didn't *rape* me." Her stomach muscles constricted as she said the R-word.

"Really?" His eyes narrowed, though his tone softened by

a fraction. "Because you're displaying the same behaviors Bri did."

"It wasn't rape," she repeated, weaker this time.

"What happened then?" He didn't back down.

Tightness in her chest rebounded quicker than it had abated. She pulled out the chair and sat, using the kitchen table as a buffer. "I met this guy while celebrating a friend's birthday at a club. We went out the next week. I found out he was in the Army over dinner, but he seemed like such a nice guy. Talked about his family and what he wanted to do when he got out of the Army."

The story came easier as Linc eased silently into the other chair, angling it so he was closer and not directly across from her.

"We went to dinner and a movie another night. Then, he invited me to a party in his apartment complex. We'd both had too much to drink to drive, so we went back to his apartment. After a while, I tried to put the brakes on things . . ." She gave minimal information.

"And he didn't take no for an answer."

"Not exactly. He said it wasn't fair because he was 'too worked up to stop.' So, I—I did what he wanted." She fought back the tears as helplessness, shame, and guilt pressed down on her like a concrete slab. "It's just as much my fault."

"No! *You* didn't do anything wrong." Linc's tone lowered the temperature in the room. "You said no. That should have been the end of it. Getting 'too worked up?' That's utter bullshit. No guy ever died from that. He could have gone and jacked off. Trust me, he does that regularly anyway. You have the right to say no—at *any* time. Even if you initially gave consent. Even if you've had sex with him before. It's your body. Pressuring you to do a sexual act against your will, minimally, it's sexual assault. Or date rape, which is still rape."

His passionate words delivered a powerful blow to the blame she'd carried since. Though it also drove home the reality she'd tried to deny. It wasn't a matter of things going too far. She had been sexually *assaulted*.

"Look at me." He paused until she did. "I'm sorry it happened to you. I've seen what it can do to a person. I don't want it to ever happen to you again or to keep screwing up your life." His voice cracked, and he broke eye contact, but not before she saw the grief in his eyes.

Clearly, he was a protector. Bri. Jalen. Even trying to protect her. "I did talk to a counselor but didn't delve into all the specifics." Since she didn't want to be told it was her fault. "Certain situations can still be triggering."

"I get that. Thank you for trusting me enough to be honest."

"I do trust you." More than she'd trusted any man since then. "We both need to get to sleep. It's been a long day." Reliving what Don had done to her had drained the little energy remaining, though, surprisingly, she was in a better frame of mind than before they had this conversation.

He nodded and didn't stop her as she retreated to the bedroom.

AFTER AN HOUR that seemed like an eternity, Kendra finally admitted defeat and got out of bed. When she cracked the bedroom door, she could make out Linc sitting on the couch, his face lit by the computer screen. His head jerked up as she drifted into the living room.

"Couldn't sleep?" she asked.

"Not when I'm no closer to finding Regina or Bri than I

was this morning. Guessing you couldn't either." He shifted on the cushion. "Sorry if I overstepped earlier."

"You didn't. I needed to hear what you said." She sat on the couch, curling a leg under her to semi-face him. "About two weeks, after—*it*, I told two of my friends. One had a similar experience in college. I guess I wanted them to tell me he was wrong, and I wasn't to blame. Instead, I came away with more of a sense of 'we put ourselves in a bad situation and decided to give in rather than stand up for ourselves.' I thought I'd be able to let it go, but . . ."

"It doesn't magically *un*happen or go away."

He was right there. Little things like his unanticipated touch earlier were reminders. "It wasn't too long after that when I met you. I was afraid of getting into a situation I couldn't control again." That night still made her distrustful—of men and herself.

"I get that." Linc nodded in a manner that reassured her he did understand—unfortunately, because of what had happened to Bri.

"It took a while to start dating, and I've only had one long-term relationship." Most guys weren't interested in taking things as slow as she needed. "Marcus was older and more mature than guys my age. When I finally told him what happened, he was understanding and patient, but he never dispelled the blame I've carried like you did tonight." She sniffed and knuckled away a tear that escaped. Normally, even thinking about it raised her anxiety, and she couldn't maintain eye contact. But Linc's early reaction validated and empowered her.

"If it weren't for what happened to Bri, I might not get it either. But I saw what it did to her. She was only twelve, and it—it tears me up that I wasn't there for her. I saw how their dealer looked at Bri, but I left to shoot hoops with the new ball they gave me." His face pinched.

"Linc, you had no way of knowing they would let that happen."

"*Let* it happen?" he scoffed. "They *sold her* so they could get high."

She didn't want to believe Bri's own parents would do that. But, in Kendra's line of work, she'd seen similar—and worse, so she didn't contradict him.

"I quit playing ball after that night and wouldn't leave her alone with them. I didn't trust them, but I didn't know what else to do to protect her or how to get her help. They died in the car accident a few months later. I tried to tell Mrs. Feldman what happened. Except, she didn't want to hear it—and admit her son pimped out his daughter for drugs. Bri never got counseling. If she had, maybe she wouldn't have turned to drugs. Just like our mom. And it's why she didn't value herself, and . . ."

Kendra laid a hand on Linc's arm. "It's *not your fault*. You were a kid. You tried to get her help. And you've been there for her when she got arrested and could have gone to jail. When she could have lost custody of Jalen. And you're here now." He'd taken leave and come all the way back here because Bri said she was in trouble. He could have blown it off. "I hope the authorities find her and she gets out of this."

"If not, I don't know what I'll do."

She'd known this was personal, with Bri being his sister. Now that she knew their history, she understood why he couldn't stay out of it and leave it to the police. She sighed. "The other thing keeping me from sleeping is that I need to apologize. I did stereotype, and I prejudged you because you're in the military. That wasn't fair, and you've opened my eyes to see that."

"Okay." His mouth quirked up in a grin that heated her up in all the right places.

"When I'm wrong, I admit it so we can put it in the past and start with a clean slate." She paused and summoned her courage. "I know the timing stinks with this situation, and you have to go back to wherever you're deployed when it's resolved, but when you get home, I'd like to take you out for dinner. Kind of my way of apologizing," she fumbled for words.

"I'm not sure that's a good idea," he said, shaking his head.

Her lungs seized. What did she expect after rejecting him? She'd taken a risk.

"I wouldn't want your family to disown you."

She couldn't tell if he was teasing or serious, but her lungs started to work again. "Maybe it's time for Grandma Ruby to be enlightened too."

He studied her silently for a few seconds. "Counteroffer. I ask you out. You accept this time. I take you to dinner, and if that goes well, *then* you can invite me to dinner."

"Technically, you've already taken me to dinner."

"You mean today? No. I *paid* for dinner, but it wasn't *a date*. So, we start over?" He held out his hand.

"Agreed." She shook his hand.

He clasped hers tighter and leaned against the back of the couch, staring intently at her. "Is it okay if we just stay here like this for a minute or two?"

"Sure." She repositioned to get comfortable, letting her shoulder and upper arm touch his. It felt surprisingly comfortable. "I guess you don't get a lot of contact and handholding when you're deployed."

He gave an amused chuckle. "Hardly." He squeezed her hand lightly and rested them atop his thigh. "I need this."

Sitting here together, simply holding hands, restored a

sense of balance and control missing from her life these past few years. She needed this, too—a man with whom she could share what she'd been through without judgment.

It'd taken weeks of dating before she'd had the courage to tell Marcus. He'd taken it well, though he hadn't reacted like she'd hoped. Not like Linc had. Not only did Linc's reaction surprise her, it made him even more attractive. And not just physically so.

She'd been able to get intimate with Marcus, though physical desire and passion hadn't been there. But she wanted that again. And Linc sent her body temperature to the you-should-be-hospitalized heat level. However, she should still take things slow.

After several minutes of sitting silently with his eyes closed, she suspected that he had dozed off. "Do you think you'll be able to sleep now?"

"There's a better chance than before you came in here." He roused himself upright and closed his laptop while holding onto her hand. "I do need to sleep if I'm going to be any good tomorrow. Thanks again. For everything." He lifted their joined hands and pressed a kiss to the top of hers.

The way he looked at her had her leaning in toward him. Except she lost her nerve and pressed a kiss to his shoulder. His fingers squeezed hers before letting go.

"Good night." His husky voice would be whispering to her in her dreams.

THIRTEEN

Linc bolted upright, looking for the source of the noise that woke him. The screen lit up as his phone vibrated on the coffee table. Still clinging to the hope that Bri would find a way to get free, his surge of adrenaline waned when he saw the call was from Walt.

"Sorry if I'm waking you," Walt said. "But the kids are up and want Jalen to go to church with us. I wasn't sure when you needed to get him."

"I hadn't thought that far, but if he wants to go with you, that'd be a help." Linc ran a hand over the back of his head, trying to shake off the remnants of a sound sleep. "I appreciate it."

"We'll trade. You can keep my three while I take Tammy on a weeklong cruise."

"Right. That sounds like a fair tradeoff." Hardly. Though, if Bri came home safely, he'd do it—with her help. They were down to two days before she was supposed to fly home. Two days to find her, or . . . Or what? Possibilities he didn't want to think about flashed across his mind. In his work, he'd seen the horrible things people did to others—not just in war.

There was no going back to sleep now, so Linc went to the kitchen. He started the coffee and set out what he needed to fix breakfast.

"Good morning. Can I help with anything?" Kendra appeared wearing Dev's T-shirt and athletic shorts, which showed off her shapely legs.

"If you want some scrambled eggs and ham, you can crack the eggs. I'll take four. Sorry if the phone call woke you."

"Clara or the police?" She started cracking eggs into a bowl.

"I wish. The Shulers. They're taking Jalen to church, so we've got the morning free." He opened the package of country ham. "The water in the pot is for your tea."

"Thank you."

The smile she aimed at him would normally have him taking things in a more romantic direction, but he wasn't going to risk moving too fast. Even though her tantalizing mouth tempted him to taste her, he settled for the slow burn of anticipation.

After she poured water into a mug and added a tea bag, she hunted in Dev's pantry for spices and seasoned the eggs while he cooked the ham. It'd been a long time since he'd cooked breakfast with a woman he hadn't slept with. Kendra had the kind of positive outlook and restraint that countered and complemented his disposition, but her family wouldn't approve if they dated. There was no point worrying about that yet.

He'd ended his last relationship when Tayshia started pushing for their fun, no-commitment arrangement to become more. Before he deployed, she'd invited her parents to meet him, telling him after the plans were made. Her parents had been on board with him being military, even Special Ops, but things got uncomfortable when her mother began asking about his parents and family. Something that he and Tayshia hadn't even discussed yet. It became clear they envisioned different futures, and she wanted things he couldn't commit to.

He'd made it into the elite Delta unit because of the men who helped mold him for that. But how could he be a good husband and father with no role models? He shouldn't waste mental energy on that when he needed to focus on finding Bri.

"I'll call Clara to see if she knows anything more and let her know which grid I plan to search today," Linc said as he carried his plate to the sink.

"I'll clean up here while you call," Kendra offered.

The line rang twice before his call was redirected to voice-mail. A message popped up on his screen.

Can't talk now. Call you shortly.

At least she wasn't totally ignoring him.

The weight on his shoulders and in his chest grew as he opened his laptop to the map. Fayetteville wasn't a big city, but even spending hours canvassing yesterday, they'd barely covered a fraction of the city. He had no idea how many license plate readers the local police had. If the guy had swapped out plates, they weren't going to get leads that way. This might be their best shot at finding Regina. But he couldn't count on her having any information on Bri's location in Mexico. They needed the guy who took her. *He* would know where they were.

By now, the police might have found a hotel reservation for Tawnya. He could leave Jalen with the Shulers and be in Mexico tonight.

With the clock ticking down, if the police hadn't learned anything, it was time to call in reinforcements. Ask Angela Hoffman to see what she could dig up.

"I'm going to get dressed so I can head out."

"I will too," Kendra offered without him asking.

He'd just emerged from the bathroom to wait for Kendra when his phone rang. "Wondered if you had any updates," he greeted Clara.

"We caught a break and think we have a location. We're waiting for a judge to grant a warrant now."

"How long will that take?"

"I don't know. It's Sunday."

"Just give me the location." He didn't need a warrant. Adrenaline pumped through him as he reached for the notepad.

"Leave this to law enforcement."

"My team and I are some of the best *in the world* at what we do. *This* kind of mission is *exactly* what we train for and execute—*successfully*. If it were Kendra or someone else you cared about, we are—I am—who you'd want going in to get them out."

"We're trained as well."

"Trust me, it's not the same."

"I understand you wanting to help, but you're too personally involved. This is *not your mission*. You are not deployed—"

"I have credentials allowing me to operate on US soil."

"You're not listening to me. At this point, we don't know that the van is there or that it's the right location."

"I have access to equipment that can tell us what type of vehicle may be housed and to determine how many people are on the premises. Where they're located inside. Sending me in covertly has a better chance of success than sending a uniformed officer to the door or rolling up with a SWAT team."

"I can't have you going vigilante and breaching some residence. I'm trying to keep you from being arrested, which won't do your sister or her grandmother any good."

"I'm not going vigilante. I want him taken into custody because he's our best—and maybe only—shot at finding Bri." Not that he'd get to participate in the interrogation.

"We want him alive, *but* recovering Mrs. Feldman is our priority. I'll give you an update once I know more." Clara ended the call.

"Dammit. They're making a mistake." A huge one. He breathed out, trying to keep from smashing something of Dev's.

Kendra hung back near the kitchen counter.

"I guess you heard that."

"Kind of hard not to. I know it's frustrating, but you need to trust that the police know what they're doing."

He shook his head. Frustrating didn't even begin to describe being shut out when they finally might be learning something. Hell yes, it was personal, but it meant he would do it the right way to bringing this guy in alive.

"Are we going out searching for the van?"

He took a moment to think. Clara mentioned a residence. They might stumble across the action if he and Kendra continued their search. Then what? If he had a pair of thermal imaging goggles, he could call Clara and offer them up so SWAT would know what they were looking at before going in. "I need to go over to post and get some things." He grabbed the car keys.

"Okay." Kendra picked up her purse.

"That part of post is restricted. You'll have to stay here."

She crossed her arms over her chest and stared at him.

"I'm serious. I would need to get authorization. By the time we do all that, I can get there and be back. You don't want to be around me right now, and I can't just sit here."

"I get that." She sighed. "Promise me you won't do anything illegal or stupid."

Hopefully, that was her way of saying she cared. "I promise." He closed the distance between them.

Resting a hand on Kendra's hip, he pressed a kiss to her forehead. "I said I'd take you to dinner. I keep my promises." Which is why he had to save Bri. He promised he wouldn't let anything happen to her again.

AFTER GOING by post and getting thermal imaging goggles as well as surveillance cameras that could snake under a door, Linc called Clara. It went straight to voicemail. Was she on another call or had she blocked him?

He gave her a few minutes to text him back before he called again. This time, when it rolled to voicemail, he left a message. He left post and headed back to Dev's. He'd just hit the garage door button when Clara called him back.

"We got the warrant. It was the right house."

Yes!

"Mrs. Feldman is shaken up and a bit disoriented, but physically not harmed. They're taking her to Med to be checked out."

"And the guy who took her?"

"He was there. He's on his way to Med with a GSW to the chest."

Fuck! He pounded his head against the headrest. "How bad?"

"It doesn't look good. He fired on one of our officers. They didn't have a choice."

Yes, they did. A shot through his gun hand or hit him in the knee. If they had let *him* go in, that's what he would have done. He kept his mouth shut since he already had a strike or two against him with Kendra's family because he served in the Army, and he didn't want to piss off a potential ally in Clara. However, if it came down to saving Bri or pleasing Kendra and her family, he'd have to do the best things for Bri and Jalen. Kendra would understand. He'd never make her alienate her family for him.

"We've got a team combing the house for information on Tawnya's and Bri's whereabouts," Clara continued.

"Was Tawnya living there?"

"Doesn't look like it. There were only men's clothes. We're running down the LLC that owns the house. Whoever rented it for him may have also rented one for Tawnya."

"Have you ID'd the guy?"

"Heath Malloy. He's got a pretty lengthy rap sheet. Mostly drug-related. Some assault charges. We questioned him a few months ago but didn't have enough evidence to make charges stick."

Evidence usually wasn't a problem with drug and assault arrests. A chill ran down Linc's spine. "What kind of charges?"

"Attempted kidnapping. It could have been a similar situation. I'm headed over to the hospital. I'm guessing you'd like to meet me there while I question Mrs. Feldman. Even though we got Malloy, you should keep your nephew someplace safe. Based on the clothing, there were two men living in the house. Right now, we don't know anything about the second's identity or whereabouts. We're running a list of his known associates and getting prints from the house to determine who else was staying there and their current location."

Shit. "Got it." He'd thought they'd caught a break learning the location where Regina was being held. Instead, they might have killed their best shot at getting Bri out of Mexico.

FOURTEEN

Since she could practically feel the tension rolling off Linc's body from the moment he'd entered the house, she opted to come along to the hospital for support. He filled Kendra in on the details he got from Clara as they drove across town.

"Did you want to pick up Jalen and take him to see his great-grandmother?" she asked.

"Not yet. I need to know what kind of condition she's in before he sees her. I can't risk her saying anything when Jalen thinks his mother is coming home in two days."

"That's a good call."

While they waited for a red light to change, his right hand tapped impatiently on his thigh. She placed her fingers on the back of his hand to calm him.

He looked into her eyes with a trace of a smile forming. "Thanks for coming," he said, interlacing his fingers with hers.

The simple touch ignited a longing for more contact. A lot more. In just a matter of days, Lincoln Porter had imploded the wall she'd erected for her protection. Even with a kidnapper potentially still on the hunt for her, she'd never felt safer than she did with Linc by her side.

Outside the ER, they found Clara seated in the waiting room.

"You didn't need to bring her here," Clara said, giving Kendra a hug.

"I volunteered."

Clara raised an eyebrow at that.

"It was come or stay at his friend's house all by myself."

"Is Jalen still with your friends?" Clara asked Linc.

"Yeah. I asked him to text when they get out of church to see if they can keep him a little longer."

"They're examining Mrs. Feldman now. They gave her a mild sedative, but I asked the nurse not to knock her out until I get a chance to speak with her." Clara sat back down, and Kendra took the seat next to her. Linc studied the waiting room before sitting on the other side of Kendra.

It took several minutes of sitting there with a home makeover show to distract them before Linc's leg bounced enough to shake Kendra's chair. She gently touched his arm and met his gaze.

"Sorry." He placed his forearms on his legs.

As he scrolled on his phone, she saw he was checking flight schedules to Acapulco. So much for letting authorities handle things. With the kidnapper being shot, that didn't surprise her.

He angled to stare Clara down. "You said she wasn't hurt. What's taking so long?"

"She was a little out of it, so they were going to do an MRI. They wanted to make sure she didn't have a TIA."

"She had a stroke?" His posture shifted.

"We don't know that. It's just a precaution," Clara assured them.

Linc took a deep breath and leaned back, resting his head against the wall as they waited. A few minutes later, his phone chimed. He got up. "I'm going outside for better reception to call Walt."

Clara gave a head nod of approval.

"What would Grandma Ruby say?" Clara smiled like the Cheshire cat at Kendra before Linc even made it from the area.

"About what?"

"Right." Clara laughed. "I saw you touch his arm and the way you looked at him. I can't say I blame you. He's yummy."

"You're married. *To my cousin*," Kendra deflected.

"I'm married, not blind. And, if I weren't married, I'd be finding a way to handcuff him to a—"

"I *do not* need to hear more." Kendra held up a hand. "Yes, I like him," she admitted. "But with this situation, the timing is hardly ideal. We'll see what happens after he finishes his deployment. So, you don't need to be saying anything to Grandma Ruby."

"I won't. He may get on my nerves by inserting himself into this investigation, but I admire his dedication. And he's wicked smart."

"He's also great with this nephew." Which was even more appealing than his looks and intelligence. If Bri landed in prison—or worse—would Linc be up to the task of being a full-time caregiver to Jalen? From everything she'd witnessed, he would, and he'd been quite adamant that he didn't want Jalen going into foster care or being adopted. What would it mean for his career in the Army? Even though it might appease Grandma Ruby if Linc left the Army, for his sake, and Bri's and Jalen's, she hoped they'd get information from Mrs. Feldman that would lead to Bri getting home safely.

"I know Grandma Ruby has her rules, but from what I've heard and seen, she's got a type, and I think it's more *her* bad taste in men than the fact some of them happened to be in the military," Clara speculated.

"Her type?" A bud of hope sprouted in Kendra's chest.

"Haven't you noticed she goes for the anti-heroes in movies? And she reads motorcycle club and mafia romances?"

"So?" Kendra hadn't thought about it from the perspective of Ruby's attraction to men.

"You always do look for the best in people. I think it's your superpower." Clara laughed. "My job makes me more jaded and notice the not-so-best. It's like Ruby thinks love can redeem the bad boy—which isn't usually the case in real life. She once asked me if I could dig up information on some men she once knew." Innuendo laced Clara's voice. "She couldn't find them on Facebook or the internet and thought I might have better luck."

"Did you?" Kendra's interest was piqued. She'd only heard stories about Ruby and the three military men in her life.

"I found one. He'd served six months in jail for stabbing someone in a bar fight. Even after I told her that, she wanted to know if I had an address for him."

"*No.*"

"I didn't give it to her, but make sure she doesn't get involved in some prison ministry writing letters because I can see where that might go."

The two laughed, and Kendra mulled over Clara's point that Grandma Ruby had poor judgment in men. While she'd made a mistake with Don, that didn't mean she was doomed to make the same mistake by dating another man in the military. Maybe Grandma Ruby needed to accept her share of the blame and butt out of other people's love lives.

There'd been no way to eavesdrop without them knowing, so Linc kept walking after overhearing Clara mention their Grandma Ruby. It didn't surprise him that not much got past the detective. And even as an in-law, that Clara knew about Ruby disapproval of military men showed it was serious.

Clara had stated Kendra was a rule follower. That likely meant they'd go on a few dates, and that would be the end, like most of his relationships. He didn't have a problem being exclusive, but when the where-do-you-see-this-relationship-going question inevitably came up, that was typically the beginning of the end—if not *the* end.

Since he didn't want anyone to feel the sting of rejection he'd experienced over and over, he let them make the call. Sometimes, he sped the end along rather than let things get complicated with too many feelings, leading to wanting things he couldn't have. If he could offer a woman more than short-term, it would be with someone like Kendra. Except her family wouldn't be on board for them being together. Since she was aware of that, maybe she was looking for something casual—or wanted to take another step in healing from her assault.

Outside the hospital, dark rain clouds hung low in the sky, fitting his mood. While he doubted anyone would show up for this Malloy guy, Linc still made sure no one was within earshot when he gave an update to Walt, who assured him Jalen was still having a great time. "He needs a sibling or some cousins," Walt teased.

"I'll bring that up to Bri when we get her back," Linc tried to stay positive. Walt was right. It certainly made life better that he and Bri had each other until they were separated. Because of their ages, he hadn't formed tight bonds with his foster siblings, and they never stayed together long enough to feel like family. Jalen needed a family.

Please let Regina know something useful.

Kendra and Clara flashed guilty smiles when he rejoined them in the waiting room. He didn't need to ask if they'd been talking about him.

"Is Jalen all right?" Kendra asked.

"Yeah. Plan is for him to stay with the Shulers. That way, I can head to Mexico once we know where Bri is. Have you heard anything from the team searching the house or credit card charges for hotels?" he asked Clara.

"Not yet. And you need to let the authorities handle this or you could both end up in jail—or the hands of the cartel. I do not have the authority to get you out."

"I know that." If only his team were here, he'd have backup to avoid both of those possibilities. But he could do this on his own. He could handle Tawnya. Even without a passport, he could get Bri out of Mexico if he had to. He just needed her location.

"Detective Lowe?" A middle-aged woman wearing a short, white lab coat over scrubs looked around.

Clara got to her feet. Linc did too.

"Mrs. Feldman's MRI is clear. There was no sign of a stroke. Dehydration could contribute to her being disoriented. We're running an IV, and we'll keep her overnight for observation since she said she doesn't have family here to look after her."

Linc started to speak up, but he couldn't volunteer to watch over Regina when he planned to be on a flight to Mexico. The hospital could keep her safe.

"I'll let you talk to her now. With what she's been through, she's pretty wrung out." The doctor motioned for them to follow her.

"I'll wait here," Kendra said.

"The guy that took her was brought in with a GSW to the

chest. Do you know if he made it through surgery?" Clara asked.

The doctor pressed the button for the elevator. "I heard the call come in. I can check and let you know after you talk with Mrs. Feldman. It's best not to say in front of her." They stopped outside a private hospital room. "I'll check and have a nurse give you an update on the shooting patient."

Inside, Regina wore a hospital gown and laid against pillows. Her eyes flew open as they entered.

Her hair was uncharacteristically unkempt. Without her usual make-up, her skin was pale, and dark circles under her eyes spoke of her terrifying ordeal. Her gaze darted from the doctor to Clara, then settled on Linc. "What are you doing here? Where's Jalen? They—"

Linc choked down the urge to defend his presence. "He's safe. He's with friends from my team."

"Thank goodness." Regina rested a hand on her chest and breathed out.

"Mrs. Feldman, I'm Detective Lowe. I'm so sorry for what you've been through, but I need to ask you some questions regarding your granddaughter."

"Bri? She's—she's in Mexico with a woman who I—I think that woman is working with the man who took me." Regina's voice warbled.

"We're aware of that," Clara said. "We retrieved a voice-mail Bri left you shortly before you were taken."

"If she'd called me, I would have answered," Regina shook her head.

"She called from a burner phone, likely belonging to whoever she was with. Do you know the name of the friend she went to Mexico with?" Clara asked.

"Tawnya something. She was emphatic about the pronun-ciation."

"Did you meet her?"

"Briefly. She stopped by the night before they left to drop off a suitcase for Bri to use."

Alarm bells pinged in Linc's brain at that information.

"Is this the woman?" Clara showed her a picture on her phone of a Caucasian woman with straight, dull brown hair.

"Yes! That's her."

"Did they give you the name of the hotel or resort where they were staying?"

"They said Acapulco. Bri showed me pictures of blue water and palm trees where they'd be staying, but I don't remember them saying a name. I'm sorry." She snuffed out Linc's sliver of hope that she knew where and that it was Bri's actual location.

"Do you know if anyone came to the house with the man who took you?" Clara continued to probe.

"There was a second man in the van. After the first night, I only heard one man's voice. And I heard what sounded like that Tawnya, but I'm sure they were on the phone. They mentioned Bri not wanting to do something. Tawnya was all fired up that he took me and didn't get Jalen. Things got real heated, and I heard him leave, but I couldn't get free." Regina rubbed the bruises on her wrist.

Linc's skin broke out in goosebumps. What if he hadn't come? Malloy could have followed Kendra and gotten to her and Jalen.

"I heard him talking to a man last night, but I think it was on the phone too. I never saw anyone else. Bri's in danger, isn't she?" Regina locked gazes with Linc.

He nodded.

"She said you were deployed to Europe."

This wasn't his fault. Why did he always feel less than

around this woman? "I was. She called, indicating she was in trouble. When I couldn't reach her, I took leave."

"You've got to get her back. Please." Tears shimmered in the woman's eyes, and her jaw trembled as her gaze shifted between Clara and Linc.

"We're working on that. If you think of anything that might be useful, call me." Clara set a business card on the hospital tray. "Get some rest."

"Lincoln, can I speak to you for a minute?" Regina looked him in the eyes rather than through him.

"I'll see about getting an update from the nurse." Clara stepped out of the room.

"Thank you for coming to help her. When your mother and Clifton died, I—I was wrong to split you and Bri up. She needed you. I didn't see it then. If I could go back in time, I'd have you live with me too. No one wants to be labeled a racist, and I could blame my upbringing, but I thought you'd be a bad influence. It's past time to apologize for being wrong about that too. I'm trying to do better, and I hope, with time, you can forgive me."

Linc swallowed the lump that had formed in his throat at the confession he never thought he'd hear from this woman. He let out a breath along with most of the resentment he'd harbored for over a decade. His life might have taken a different path if it weren't for her. But would it have been better? Was it all part of a cosmic plan meant to put him here today with the skills to rescue Bri?

"I've resented you for that," he admitted. "But I'm willing to put the past behind us and start again."

Regina sniffed, and fat tears rolled down her wrinkled cheeks. "I should have had the courage to say all that years ago." She gave a weak smile. "It feels like a weight's been lifted."

He nodded in agreement. Even if she didn't have information to help with his mission, they were family because they both loved Bri and Jalen.

"Bri's so proud of you. Says you're in one of those special units that can't talk about what you do in the Army." She studied his face when he didn't confirm or deny her statement. "I hope it's true and you get her back because if she doesn't do what they want, I think they'll do something horrible to her."

"I'm going to do everything I can. I need to go now."

"Be careful."

He started to respond with *I always am*, like he would say to Bri, but, coming from her, the warning made him hesitate. As personal as this mission was, he was on his own and needed to be cautious.

In the hallway, he spotted Clara waiting near the nurses' station. "What'd you find out?"

"He's still in surgery. It doesn't sound like we'll be talking to him for a while—if at all. I'm going back to the precinct to see what we can get from the phones we found at the house— if we can access them."

"Bring the phones here. If he used biometrics, we use his prints, facial recognition, or scan his iris to access it. Since you have proof of the kidnapping, I'm sure you can get a warrant."

"Good idea. A patrol officer is coming to provide security outside Mrs. Feldman's room. I'll have him bring the phones over so we can try unlocking them." Clara was already placing the call.

"Was she able to tell you anything useful?" Kendra asked when they rejoined her in the waiting room.

"Not really," Clara said. "Other than being a bit traumatized, she wasn't injured."

"I'm sorry she didn't know where Bri is," Kendra said to him.

"I figured her knowing the location was a longshot." With Malloy in surgery, his phone could be their only shot at getting that information.

In less than twenty minutes, a uniformed officer arrived and handed the phones to Clara. For the next half hour, Kendra kept a list while he and Clara tried passcodes before getting locked out.

"Let's take a break and get some coffee while we wait for the lockout to end or for him to get out of surgery," Clara suggested.

Despite years of experience waiting days and even weeks to execute a mission, this was excruciating. If he couldn't get on one of today's afternoon flights to Acapulco, the morning flight wouldn't get him there until nearly five tomorrow afternoon. He hadn't realized it'd take nearly twelve hours to travel on commercial flights to Acapulco from here. That left him fifteen hours at best to find Bri and get her away from Tawnya and anyone else who could be holding her.

A surgeon in scrubs and skull cap entered the waiting room. "Detective Lowe?"

Clara stepped over to speak with him.

Linc edged close enough to hear that Malloy survived the surgery. Then Clara launched into her explanation of why she needed to see his patient now.

"Come with me." The surgeon didn't even hesitate.

Clara motioned for Linc to join them.

"Give the detectives a minute with the patient," the surgeon instructed the post-op nurse inside the recovery room as he removed the tape from Malloy's eyes.

Please let this work. Linc pressed Malloy's finger to the screen. The home screen appeared. "Thank you," he whispered, then swapped phones with Clara and accessed the second.

"We need to get these to the tech."

"Why not check them here?"

"We can't risk losing information or breaking the chain of custody."

He exhaled through clenched teeth and checked that they were sufficiently charged. Without the passcode or supplies to clone Malloy's fingerprint, the last thing he needed was for them to die or time out. Not when he needed every minute.

"You drive." He handed the keys to Kendra in the waiting room so he could manage to keep both phones active on the drive to the police station.

After they were passed off to a tech, they went back to waiting mode. Fortunately, it wasn't but half an hour before the tech called them into his workspace.

"He was smart enough to delete messages, but he didn't delete the cache, so I could retrieve everything from the past week. Based on the voicemail and text messages, they kept the phones turned off most of the time. I noted the time and length of the phone calls. They were only between four numbers, and one of those was a local Chinese restaurant."

"That tracks with the delivery cartons found on scene," Clara said.

"I cloned the sim card in his phone. This will get any calls or texts to his numbers, but you won't need a passcode to access it." He handed Clara a cell phone and a printout. "I put the texts and voicemails in chronological order. Start with the first recorded message. You'll be able to follow what's going on quite clearly." His tone added more weight to Linc's shoulders.

Clara played the message. Linc recognized the woman's voice as the one interrupting Bri when she called him.

"We have a problem. Somehow, she got wise to the switch on the suitcase. I offered to pay her for carrying. I've locked her passport in the safe and even showed her the picture of her kid, but she's *not* cooperating. Bitch lifted my phone. She called her grandmother and warned her. You need to stake out Bri's apartment and get them before she can get the kid and disappear."

"Malloy texted back a half hour later." The tech pointed to the string of text messages.

> You want me to snatch her grandma and the kid

> Are you nuts?

> She'll cooperate if we have them.

> That's a lot of risk I'm not getting paid to take

> Think about the alternative if we don't deliver or lose a shipment this size

Unfortunately, they knew better than to mention who they worked for in the texts. It would have given them some information to work with.

> Her Grams drives the bright blue Toyota SUV with Georgia plates

> You need to go now

"That was the end of their conversation. Next were those text messages." The tech referenced the sheet.

> I got the old lady.

What about the kid?

"Then there's a four-minute phone call between these same numbers. Since it was live, I don't have info on that," the tech stated.

"Probably the call Mrs. Feldman mentioned overhearing." Linc imagined Tawnya giving him hell for grabbing Regina before picking up Jalen. Thank God for that miracle.

"She sent the next text a few hours later."

Did you get the kid?

Working on it

Couldn't get in daycare

Black woman picked him up

Followed them to restaurant

"Then, about a half hour later, he texted this."

Lost her. Have her plate #. Sending it to Taz to run.

"If he had followed me to Bri's . . ." Kendra shivered.

"He would have had to deal with me." Linc had been on alert because of Bri's phone call and Regina being missing, but he'd been unarmed.

"He texted the picture of Mrs. Feldman to the number." The tech moved quickly past the photo of Regina tied to a chair. "The next texts were from another number. Probably this Taz because it's, um, Ms. Andrews name, address, and that she's a social worker."

"Just like that? He found out who I am and where I live

and work?" Kendra's voice shook. "You were right about me not going back to work or home."

Linc placed a hand on her lower back, and she leaned closer. He wouldn't let them get to her any more than he'd let them get to Jalen.

The next texts involved Malloy saying she didn't have the boy with her, and Tawnya replying that Kendra would know where the kid was but not to take a risk in daylight. Later that night, he'd messaged that Kendra's car was at her apartment but that she didn't appear to be home.

"Didn't you have a surveillance camera put up?" Linc asked Clara.

"I did. Its motion activated, and I haven't seen anything suspicious," she said. "I'll review it again, but he might have kept clear and looked for lights on."

"This voicemail came in this morning." The tech hit play.

"So much for loving her Grams. She's still not cooperating. You're gonna have to get her kid. We have him, and she'll do it. She's a one-and-done. Maybe none-and-done. We could have had some fun here. Instead, she's ruined this trip. But, if you can't get the kid by tonight, I'm not risking her narcing us out. I'll get an experienced courier for this size load. It'll cost as much as I can get selling this pain in my ass to Inez."

"What does that mean?" Kendra asked.

"That they'll sell her to sex traffickers." Linc didn't sugarcoat it. He couldn't deny the reality pounding in his brain. He didn't have time to get to Mexico and save Bri.

FIFTEEN

"We got a match on prints from the house." Officer Logan read off the computer screen. "Randy Spivey. Younger than Malloy. No real record, but he's been traveling to Mexico regularly."

"Probably running the same scam as Tawnya with finding unsuspecting mules. See if you can get a location on him. If he's here and goes back to the house, he could alert Tawnya." Clara didn't need to finish her thought.

Linc had called Angela Hoffman and looped her in. So far, her contacts hadn't turned up anything new on Tawnya or Heath Malloy. For the past hour, he, Kendra, Clara, and Clara's partner had called hotels in Acapulco on the off chance they'd find a reservation in Tawnya's name. They'd called over a hundred hotels. The futility grew heavier with each call.

The clone of Malloy's phone vibrated a short while later. "Another text from Tawnya asking for an update," Linc announced. "I need to walk around for a few minutes and think." He'd been spinning up plan B while making the phone calls, but he needed to concentrate.

Under the cloudy sky, he hoofed it around the police station's parking lot, working through scenarios. He'd been totally focused on getting to Mexico to save Bri personally. Now he knew that wasn't going to happen. This time, it was he who was wrong. He hadn't listened when Dev or Clara suggested the option he kept circling back to. Bri's best option was to save herself.

He racked his brain, trying to think of a way he could communicate that to her and let her know she'd be okay.

Duh! He had made this too complicated. Bri needed to see they had Jalen. They could make a video and work something in. However, Malloy's unconsciousness in a hospital bed presented a problem, as Tawnya would expect to talk with him, even see him.

But Clara said they'd interrogated him. What if . . . That could work. It was their best shot.

He jogged to the entrance and into the squad room. "You said Malloy was questioned recently. Did you record that?"

"We always do," Clara answered.

"Do you still have the recording?"

"We should. Why?"

"Because I've got a software program that can clone his voice. We've used it in the field successfully. We can even use images to create a filter to make it look like him on the screen. We make Tawnya think Malloy has Jalen, so Bri will agree to smuggle the drugs."

"That could work," Clara agreed. "How long will it take to do the cloning? We don't want her getting impatient."

"Not long. If you can cut out everything but him speaking, that will save time, and the longer the clip we give it, the better it'll match. I'll need to listen to him to make sure I sound and speak like him, or we'll blow this. But if Bri knows

Jalen's safe with me and that we know what's going on, she'll do what they want, and we get her back here."

"If she thinks they have her son, she'll do what they want. She might try to escape or fight," Clara reasoned.

"Bri won't fight for herself." How he wished she would, but she never had. "She will, however, fight for Jalen. She'll come here."

"And Jalen's what, four? You can't rely on him not to say the wrong thing," Clara pointed out.

"True." He hadn't figured that part out yet. But Bri had to know Linc had come. That he'd help save her.

"And Mrs. Feldman's in the hospital. What if Tawnya asks about her?" Clara continued to shoot holes in his plan.

"They're looking for me to get to Jalen, right?" Kendra said. "We make her think he got both of us, and I can convey the message."

"If she asks about Mrs. Feldman, I say I'm keeping them separated because that would be smarter than putting them all together," Linc solved that problem.

"But how will you let Bri know that you're here without tipping off Tawnya?"

"This." He pulled the black geometric stone on a leather cord from under his shirt. "If Bri sees it, she'll know that I'm here."

"Why's that?" Clara asked.

"She got the set for us after Mom and her dad died. There's a magnet in each. You put them together, and they form a heart. This is my half. Hers is silver." He didn't take his off.

"All right. We can alert TSA and Homeland Security. Have them ask officials in Mexico to let them through security, and then we track Tawnya with the suitcase full of drugs to whoever she's working for and take them down. We explain

Bri is only doing this under duress, and they could catch the real players, and Bri shouldn't face any charges. I'll go to bat for her," Clara said.

"I need to get my computer. You get that interrogation footage, and contact HSI." His heart pounded with renewed hope. This could work. It had to.

BY THE TIME Linc returned to the station, the tech had distilled a copy of the interrogation recording to just Malloy. Clara gave him an office to work in where he uploaded the file for the program to run on his computer. Then, the two watched the video of Malloy's interrogation, making notes of specific word choices and speech patterns.

The cloned phone rang just as Linc got deep into character as Malloy. Rather than answer, he texted.

> Can't talk here

> Where the hell have you been

> Working on getting the kid

> I'm close

Close enough to give the program a run-through. He recorded a sample and viewed it, then made some tweaks to the timing.

This could work, especially if he limited his screen time and audio to focus on showing Jalen and let Kendra plead with Bri. He loaded the filters onto his phone and called Kendra in.

He took off his necklace and fastened it around her neck. "I'm gonna want this back."

"I figured you would." She touched the stone with her fingertip. "You're a remarkable man and brother, Linc Porter."

"I don't know about that." He'd let Bri down, and he couldn't afford to let her down again.

"Trust me, in my line of work, I see a lot of things. Bri has turned things around—in large part because of you. And you're an amazing uncle to Jalen."

"That part's easy. Bri's the one carrying the load with all she does for him." Though Kendra saying that, and the way she stared into his eyes, instilled a sense of value and worth that ignited the longing he had worked to suppress. He would have kissed her right here if Clara hadn't been standing a few feet away.

"Let's give it a try live. I'll call your cell and see if it looks and sounds convincing," he said to Clara before addressing Kendra. "We're just going to do one run-through because we don't want you to sound rehearsed. You should sound nervous and scared. But it's important to draw attention to the necklace. If you do that when you tell her it will be okay to do what they want, she *should* get the message."

After a successful run-through with Clara calling Linc's transformation to look and sound like Malloy as scarily realistic, it was time to do this for real. Linc messaged Walt to have him bring Jalen to meet them at the house where Malloy had held Regina.

They drove to just outside the city on a road where the homes were spaced far enough away from neighbors to provide privacy, though they'd surely noticed the earlier police presence. If Malloy had a partner who drove by then or now, this whole plan would tank.

A chill gripped Linc the moment he walked in, despite the home's normal appearance. Kendra kept close to his side, as if she felt the darkness too.

"It's likely Tawnya's been here before," Clara said as they passed through the foyer. "He kept Mrs. Feldman in the walk-in closet in the main bedroom. We need to use another room for Kendra and Jalen."

"Nice. Stick an old woman in a dark closet," Linc muttered.

"If Malloy survives, he'll be spending decades in a cell. No way he's skating, even if he cooperates."

"Good," Kendra said, eyeing Linc like she could guess what he'd like to do to Malloy if he walked free.

They checked out the other bedrooms.

"This one works. I'll film you and Jalen on the futon there." Thankfully, they wouldn't be real hostages—which could have happened. That thought ripped through him. If he'd blown off Bri's message or the chief hadn't let him come, Jalen could have been taken. What would Bri's chances of getting home have been then? She'd sacrifice herself, even her grandmother, for Jalen. Now, she needed to know it was safe to go along with the smuggling plan.

Walt arrived with Jalen a few minutes later.

"Missed you, J-man." Linc lifted him into his arms. "I appreciate you and Tammy helping out."

"Happy to. He's good at following orders, so he's welcome anytime." Walt and Jalen exchanged a salute.

"I'll let you know." With Walt now in a non-deploying position, if this play didn't work to get Bri home safely, or she ended up facing charges and jail time in Mexico, maybe the Shulers would consider fostering Jalen. They'd let Linc see him and stay involved in his life. He prayed it didn't come down to it, but it would be a loving home where he'd have family and stability, which was more than Linc could give him.

"Beckham's my new friend. We went to the park bof days. I hurt my knee." Jalen pointed to the bandage.

"Sorry about that," Walt said. "No stitches needed, so I didn't call."

"No worries. You're tough like me, right?" Linc tickled Jalen's tummy.

"Tough guys." Jalen flexed his little bicep.

"See you again soon." Walt gave Jalen a fist bump in farewell, both adding the finger waggle explosion.

"We're going inside and see Ms. Kendra for a minute. I'm going to make a video of her, and I need you to sit with her but not say anything. Can you do that for me?"

"Why?"

"I need to send it to somebody."

"To Mommy?"

"Yes."

"I wanna tell her I miss her." Jalen teared up, his tough guy façade crumbling in seconds.

"You can tell her that at the end." He couldn't risk Jalen mentioning Uncle Linc being here, so recording it would be the safest option versus live. He took Jalen inside before the hole in his chest expanded. Maybe he wasn't meant to have his own family, but he would do whatever it took to protect Jalen and Bri.

After Jalen showed Kendra the bandage on his knee, Linc got them on the futon.

Once he positioned himself to film, Jalen smiled big and waved to the camera. That wasn't going to work. "Pretend I'm a scary monster," Linc said.

Instead of looking scared, Jalen pretended to shoot him with an imaginary gun. In other circumstances, it might have been cute. However, cute was the antithesis of what he was going for here. He didn't want to have to tie up and blindfold his nephew.

"How about you pretend Uncle Linc told you that you can't watch your show and you don't get a snack," Kendra suggested.

That worked.

"Keep that face on, J-man, and let Miss Kendra talk."

Kendra wrapped her arms protectively around Jalen and projected the perfect terrified expression.

He pressed record and gave her the go signal.

"Bri, we know what they want you to do, and that you don't want to." Kendra's voice shook convincingly, and she touched Linc's half of the heart necklace. "If you do it, then we'll be all right, and you will too. You *need* to do what they want."

"I miss you, Mommy. Come home soon," Jalen piped in with the perfect timing.

"Give me a minute," he stepped out and replayed the video for Clara.

"You couldn't ask for anything better. Let's keep them here while you send that to Tawnya in case she wants more."

In a perfect world, he could send the video without using the program to impersonate Malloy, but he didn't bank on that happening as he typed out a message.

Mission accomplished.

He didn't expect an immediate response, but one minute turned to two to three.

Inside the bedroom, Kendra played a game on her phone

with Jalen while Linc continued to stare at Malloy's phone in his hand. When it finally rang, he startled. Seeing it wasn't a video like he'd feared, he activated the voice filter before answering. "That work?"

"It did. Just in time."

"Good. I'm taking a lot of risk here."

"She's definitely a one-and-done. I'll take her with me to the delivery. We won't have to worry about her after that."

Linc's blood froze in his veins. Malloy would know what that meant. Linc could only guess—and he sure as hell didn't like his guess. "And these three?"

"We need them for now. She wants them at the airport before turning over the suitcase."

"I'm not bringing three people to the airport."

"Just bring the kid. Do whatever you want with the other two. He's the one that matters. We'll move to our next location early. You and I can get set up, and Randy can come when he's done with his next delivery. We're almost there." She ended the call.

"You got that, right?" he asked Clara through gritted teeth.

"I did."

"We can't let Bri leave the airport with Tawnya."

"I'll reach out to my contact at HSI. We'll come up with a plan. And it's not 'we.' *You* cannot be at the airport. Tawnya knows Bri has a brother. If she knows what you look like and spots you, you'll blow the op."

"But if they're in the airport, Tawnya won't be armed."

"She's just one piece of this. Who knows how many people like her and Randy are running the same play, possibly targeting single moms. We need to aim higher if we're going to make a difference and get the major players."

"I get where you're coming from, but I'm not offering up my sister as a sacrifice for the greater good."

"That is not my intention. I'm asking you to let us come up with a plan that protects Bri but gives us enough solid evidence that Tawnya can't walk away with a deal. I want her doing serious time."

"Agreed." The bitch deserved every bit of bad karma coming her way.

"Until we learn if Spivey is here or out of the country, I need you watching over Jalen and Kendra, not locked up for interfering with a police investigation. Why don't you take Jalen to the hospital to see his great-grandmother?"

He'd experienced getting the brush off enough over the years to know now wasn't the time to push. While he doubted she'd really lock him up, he needed to show he could be a team player if he wanted her to share their plan for protecting Bri so he could evaluate any action he might need to take. "I'm trusting you," he warned before opening the bedroom door. He motioned to Kendra and Jalen.

"I haf to go to the bathroom." Jalen pulled up the front of his shorts.

"Of course you do. Is it okay to use one here?" Linc asked Clara.

"Yeah, they've processed the entire scene."

"Will you come wif me? Jalen asked Linc. "I don't like it here."

KENDRA WATCHED Jalen take Linc's hand, and the two disappeared into the bathroom. Even Jalen picked up on the vibe in the house. "Am I free to go home now?" she asked Clara.

"I'm afraid not until we know where Spivey is. He could be looking for you, and we don't know if Tawnya will relay our claim that Malloy got you both. I don't think it'll be too much of a hardship for you to be stuck with your sexy protector a little while longer."

"You don't need to do me any favors."

"I'm not. I can see you two are on the same page. He really is good with Jalen too." Clara leaned closer. "I know that's a plus in your book," she said lowly. "You give Grandma Ruby a great grandbaby, and she might overlook him being military."

"I don't know about that. Why don't you work on that great-grandbaby stuff since he and I haven't even been on a date."

"We are working on it. Well, just having fun practicing for now. You could use a little more fun in your life."

It had been months since she'd ended things with Marcus, and they hadn't had much fun in bed. Thinking about Linc had her longing for the kind of 'fun' Clara referred to. That, in and of itself, was a good turnaround.

The toilet flushed. Linc's clear reminder to Jalen to wash his hands made her wonder how much of her and Clara's conversation he overheard.

Which was worse, the sexy protector part or Clara outing how much she wanted kids before they had even kissed? Though, damn, she wanted to kiss him. And for him to kiss her in a way that wouldn't be appropriate in front of his nephew. Thinking about it, her body tingled in all the right places in a way it hadn't in—probably ever.

Linc opened the bathroom door. "I want to take him to the hospital to see his Grams. You don't mind, do you?"

"Not at all. That's thoughtful of you. I'm sure a visit from him will be better than medicine."

"Call me after you talk with Homeland Security. I need to know that plan," Linc said to Clara.

"Call me if Mrs. Feldman remembers anything useful," Clara countered.

"I will. We're a team—whether you like it or not." Linc didn't back down as he met Clara's direct gaze, exuding confidence that made Kendra glad they were on the same team.

SIXTEEN

While Linc took Jalen up to see his Grams, Kendra emailed her clients to reschedule her Monday appointments. She hated to do that when it seemed unlikely that any of Tawnya's associates would know how to find her on a client visit. She'd been verbally threatened at least a half dozen times in her six years on the job. The only time she had been physically threatened was when a parent pulled a knife on her. Understanding they were desperate, she hadn't felt truly in danger, though she had left and came back with a police officer.

This was different. Members of a drug cartel knew where she lived and where she worked. Would they just move on or blame her for having a part in busting up their operation after Malloy, Tawnya, and hopefully whoever was above her were arrested?

Linc made her feel safe, but he'd head back to Europe to finish his deployment after this week—unless they didn't get Bri back safely. Then what? Maybe she'd ask Linc to give her a self-defense lesson and tips.

She finished rescheduling and started reviewing her emails when Linc's rich laugh drew her gaze to his approach. She didn't know what he and his nephew were talking about, but the sight of them together made her heart beat faster. As good and protective as he was with his nephew, she could imagine what kind of father he would be.

"Was it good to see Grams?" She put her phone back in her bag, hoping Linc didn't see the effect he had on her.

Jalen nodded. "She needs to rest more, so she can't go home wif us."

"Is she doing better?" She asked Linc.

"They still have her on sedatives, so she's a little loopy, but seeing Jalen calmed her and should help her sleep. I thought we'd go back to the house and fix some dinner there. I'm not sure how long this one will last tonight." He placed a hand on Jalen's shoulder and turned him around to exit the waiting area.

"Did you find out anything about Malloy?"

"I asked, but they wouldn't give me any information. I figure Clara can find out."

On the short drive back to Devin's, they played a game of I Spy that became comical, since by the time Jalen picked an item, it was usually in the rearview mirror.

When they got to the house, Linc started a bath for Jalen. While Kendra boiled water for mac and cheese, she made sandwiches.

"Have anything that needs to be washed? His clothes are kind of ripe." Linc dug into the black gym bag he'd brought in the first night here and removed his dirty clothes.

She added her laundry to the washer, trying not to get too comfortable with this cozy, domestic scene. Her ex, Marcus, had spoiled her with nice dinners and gifts, but he never offered to wash her clothes, or asked about her coffee preference, or even remembered that she didn't drink coffee. But he'd been safe for her. Safe in ways that her attraction to Linc wasn't.

What Linc said the other night gave her the confidence that things could be different with him. And, unlike Marcus, who did not know how to interact with or want children, Linc was a natural with them, which made him even more desirable. She listened to Jalen giggling in the bathroom as Linc dried him off.

She got out the dinner plates and served up the sandwiches, fruit, baby carrots, and mac and cheese. Jalen darted out of the bathroom wearing the new pajama set Linc had purchased when they'd shopped at the Post Exchange the other day. Had that only been yesterday? Being with Linc around the clock the past few days blurred time.

Jalen's face lit up as he climbed onto the chair with a pillow serving as a booster seat. He didn't wait for his uncle before picking up his fork and digging into the macaroni and cheese.

"Thanks for fixing dinner." Linc took a seat. Unlike Jalen, he ate everything except the mac and cheese she'd put on his plate.

"I didn't ask if you wanted mac and cheese. Too many carbs or too processed?"

"It's not that. It's just, um, well, I've eaten enough boxed mac and cheese for three lifetimes."

"Oh." She hadn't thought about that.

"My mom left home as a teen. She didn't know how to cook and didn't have money, so we ate a lot of mac and cheese. And baloney and cheese, and grilled cheese sandwiches."

"The government free cheese program?" she asked.

"I'm not knocking it. We also had condensed chicken noodle soup weekly. Peanut butter and jelly sandwiches, hot dogs, and lots of cereal, though we didn't always have milk, and it's not the same with water. We had a neighbor down the hall, Mrs. Shannon, who lost her son. I'm sure she saw Mom slide deeper into her addiction. Mrs. Shannon claimed she had trouble getting up the three flights of stairs and sometimes would pay me a few dollars to get her groceries. Then she'd make enough to feed Bri and me dinner. She even taught me how to cook a few things.

Kendra took it as a compliment that Linc felt safe enough to share more from his past with her. It was a bonus that it provided more insight to both him and Bri. It made sense why he would have bought so much food for now, saying he could take it to Bri's.

"She sounds like an angel." She'd seen similar situations with her clients. Not many kids were lucky enough to have an angel like Mrs. Shannon. They certainly had a rough childhood, but joining the Army had not only provided for Linc financially but given him stability, a sense of worth, and even family. All good things for a young man who'd been in foster care. Some of her coworkers were advocates for kids aging out of foster care joining the military. She hadn't been due to her ingrained biases, but that would change going forward.

"You have to try a bite, or you don't get dessert." Jalen waved a fork at the pile of mac and cheese still on Linc's plate. "That's the rule."

"Maybe I don't want dessert," Linc retorted, sounding like a child himself and making a face. "Fine." Linc continued his childlike act and took a bite of mac and cheese. "Better than I remember." He ate another bite. "I might be able to eat it again. Just please don't serve me bologna and cheese."

"I promise." Kendra couldn't help but chuckle. For some reason, she'd expected a guy serving in one of the most elite military units to be intense and lack a sense of humor. Linc was definitely intense, which was warranted considering the current situation, but his sense of humor was another highly appealing quality.

"Do you want your dessert now?" Linc asked Jalen.

"Can we watch some shows, then have dessert?"

"You can watch *one* show, then it's bedtime."

Jalen placed his plate and empty milk glass on the counter near the sink. "See? I help."

"That doesn't mean you get to watch more shows." Linc got up from the table.

"More ice cream?" Jalen aimed his adorable smile at his uncle.

"Maybe bigger scoops, but you have to give me bigger hugs."

Jalen raced the three steps over to Linc, nearly toppling him as he wrapped his arms around Linc's legs.

"Thanks." Linc bent over to rub Jalen's back. "Let me help clean up, and we'll pick a show."

"I can do the cleanup," she offered.

"If I have to watch a kids' show, you do too."

"You laughed at something in it the other night."

"That was because he laughed. It's contagious."

"A child's laughter is the best sound in the world. I need to give this back to you." She reached up and unclasped the necklace she still wore and placed it in his hand.

"I hope she saw this." He fumbled with the clasp and then brought the ends around to the front to look at them.

"Let me." She took it from him. As she reached to fasten the clasp, Linc's hands rested lightly on her hips. She gave into the impulse to meet his gaze, tilting her head as his face drew closer.

"Are you coming, Uncle Linc?" Jalen called.

Linc's frustrated grumble matched the wave of disappointment crashing over her. Jalen might be adorable, but his timing sucked.

"We'll pick this up later," Linc promised in a husky, low tone.

She certainly hoped so. Though he released his hold on her, she still felt his electrifying touch.

Linc carried a kitchen chair over and resurrected the blanket fort. After he started the show, he sat close to her on the couch. When he held out his hand palm up, she put hers in his, thrilling in the simple pleasure of the light caress of his thumb.

"When is this deployment supposed to end?"

He flinched, and his grip on her hand tightened ever so slightly. "About ten weeks."

"What's it like there now?"

"We're training, not engaged in combat, so you don't need to worry about me. Most of the Ukrainian draftees barely know how to fire a weapon. They don't have much of a choice but to defend their country. It's far from ideal. They have to provide their own gear, and they're sent into the field after a few weeks. We do what we can to give them a fighting chance, but . . ." he trailed off.

"That's got to be hard."

"It is. A lot are my age and older. They have families and kids. Most Americans have no idea what it's like to live in a war-torn country. I don't enjoy fighting or war. I do what I do because we have enemies. That means we need a strong, prepared military to make countries think twice about bringing the fight here—or doing another attack like 9/11."

"What made you want to join Special Forces?"

"It wasn't my original plan. I wanted to do computers and cyber security to give me skills I could take into the private sector. Besides, historically, the make-up of Special Forces isn't very diverse."

"I've heard that."

"They began actively recruiting minorities with certain skills and performance scores. That they thought I could go toe-to-toe with the best of the best, just being asked to go through the selection process was affirmation like I'd never had in my life. I wanted to prove I was worthy of the chance. I contacted a former teammate who'd made it through Selection and the Q Course and asked him to mentor me."

"Smart. I understand the majority don't pass the qualification course."

"It takes a lot more than physicality. It requires endurance, the ability to think outside the box, mental and emotional stamina, and tenacity—though they make you want to quit. And you have to be a team player. Many of the ones who come in thinking they're going to beat everyone to prove they are the best don't make it through. And I could have easily been one of those washouts without Mack's insights and guidance. Serving with the men I do is a game and life changer."

Jalen crawled out of the fort and over to the sofa. "I can't hear my show."

"Sorry, J-man. We'll stop talking." Linc pulled Jalen onto the couch, where he cuddled up against Linc's side and then shifted to lay his head on Linc's leg. Linc rubbed his back. Within minutes, Jalen's eyes closed.

"There's something about the innocence of a sleeping child." Linc said, looking at his nephew.

"I know what you mean. You should get some rest too."

"I'll sleep when Bri's back home."

"There's nothing more you can do tonight to help her, and what you did today was brilliant. I know it's hard to wait and not know what is going on, but I believe it will work, and Bri will be the one snuggled up with her son two nights from now."

"I hope you're right. And that they get whoever is at the top of this food chain, so neither Bri nor Regina have to testify in court."

Kendra hadn't thought about that. "What would happen if they have to?"

"They could be targeted to keep them from testifying." He rested his head against the top of the couch. "There's even a remote chance they would have to go into Witness Protection." He exhaled noisily.

"Witness protection? You think that could happen?" That possibility hadn't occurred to her.

"Potentially."

"For how long?"

"I don't know. Whatever would be too long." His voice cracked as he lightly stroked Jalen's head.

The implications of what that would mean for Jalen getting the services he needed, as well as separating Linc from his sister and nephew, sucked the air from her chest. No wonder he was more focused on getting her home than bringing down the cartel. "Why don't you put Jalen in the bed for now? Then you and I can *talk* without disturbing him."

"Talk?" Based on the way his lips curled into a sexy smile, they were thinking some of the same things.

"We did get interrupted before." Staying in the living room was a safer alternative than inviting him to the bedroom.

He tucked one of the pillows under Jalen's head as he maneuvered from underneath, then lifted him in both arms.

The moment Linc disappeared into the bedroom, her stomach began doing acrobatics. She took two deep breaths. *You can trust him. You can trust him.*

She went to the kitchen and filled a glass with water.

Linc joined her a minute later. "We'll see if I can move him later without waking him because he'll want ice cream and might be up for another hour or three." He rolled his shoulders and popped his neck.

"Your muscles a little tight?"

"Between the flight, sleeping on the couch, and the stress, more than a little." He reached to knead the area between his neck and shoulder.

"Sounds like you could use a shoulder massage."

"If you are offering, I would lo—" he paused, "I would gladly take you up on that."

"Have a seat here." She touched the nearest kitchen chair.

He moved closer. Rather than sit, he stared into her eyes, the smile on his face melting her fears. He angled his head, and just when she thought he would kiss her, he took a seat. Her heart pounded, and she had to make an effort to breathe —but all in a good way.

His shoulders relaxed as her thumbs worked on knots near the base of his skull. "That feels good."

She applied pressure to the sides of his neck with her fingers. His shirt gaped. She could only make out what looked like the furry ears of a dog tattooed high on his back, though she wanted to see what was hidden under his T-shirt. The feel of his solid muscles under her hands as she massaged his shoulders and back ignited the need in her. Locating another knot, she used her elbow to dig into it. He winced.

"Let me know if it's too hard."

"I can take it. You are good at this."

"I'm not trained, but my cousins used to beg me and my sister to give them massages after ball practice."

"Ah, I think you got it." He rotated his shoulder. "But you don't have to stop."

"I wasn't planning to yet." Not when every inch she touched was firm and muscled. She ran her palms down his biceps, imagining doing so from a front-facing position. Him, shirtless. The tingling sensation he prompted became a full-on electrical current and sent energy to every erogenous zone in her body.

She wanted to touch him everywhere. And do more than touch. None of her prior relationships came close to this level of physical chemistry. Before she lost control and crossed some line, she tapped his shoulders. "I hope that helped."

"It did. Thanks." He rose from the chair. Turning, he captured her hand and studied her face.

"Would you kiss me already? Please." The smile that broke across his handsome face made her all the more desperate to discover if kissing him in real life would match her imagination.

"Definitely."

That one word, spoken in a soft, confident timbre, was probably the sexiest sound she'd ever heard.

Anticipation built as he raised a hand and gently tilted her face up. His other hand slid low on her hip. Resting her hands on his biceps gave her a sense of remaining in control and kept space between their bodies, for now. Their lips met at the perfect angle.

And everything about the kiss was perfect. Pressure that wasn't too little or too much. Maybe it didn't last long enough, but she wouldn't complain when he immediately followed with another kiss. When his tongue traced her lips, her tongue met his to give her a taste that made her want more.

More kisses. More bodily contact. More Linc.

His fingers tightened on her hip. She breathed out a pleasured murmur as their upper bodies made contact. Their shirts did little to subdue the scorch of his body heat. Or maybe her body was on fire.

"Let's move to the couch." He lightly gripped her hand. "Remember, you are free to stop anytime," he promised.

He hadn't needed to repeat it. That he did gave her the added reassurance to continue. She had no idea how he was still single, but she thanked the heavens that he was, despite the circumstances bringing them together. If Bri didn't get back safely, would she be a reminder of that, which could strain or even kill their shot at a relationship? Fortunately, she was an optimist and believed Clara and Linc's plan would work to get Bri out of Mexico and out of trouble with both the law and smugglers.

Hopefully, she was right because the way Linc kissed her and made her feel heard and respected was everything Kendra wanted from a man. Surely, her family and Grandma Ruby would see his character and accept him. She'd been wrong to let her grandmother's prejudices and stereotyping control who *she* dated. That was changing.

SEVENTEEN

When his phone rang, they jolted apart like teenagers caught making out by their parents. Though kissing and some light touching was as far as things had gone. "It's Clara." Not great timing, but she could have crucial intel. "Have you got an update?" he asked.

"We learned that Spivey flew to Mexico Friday. We found a hotel reservation in his name. However, there's no reservation at that hotel under any name that we can tie to Tawnya. We sent pictures of her and Bri to the hotel manager, but none of the staff recognized them as guests."

"Damn it." Linc's jaw locked, and he pounded a fist against the arm of the sofa.

"I know. But we did catch another break. We found another house owned by the same LLC as the house where Malloy and Spivey stayed. Two officers did a drive-by. Bri's car is there, which means Tawnya drove to the airport."

"I don't see how that's good since Bri will get in the car with her, and Tawnya's not planning on taking Bri back to her house to get her car." He couldn't shake Tawnya's comment to Malloy.

Kendra laid a hand on his arm. He covered her hand and gripped it with his. He didn't have his team. Or control. Without Kendra keeping him grounded, he'd be completely off the rails. "What is your plan?"

"The plan is to have a Homeland agent pull Bri for inspection once they arrive in Raleigh."

"Why not arrest Tawnya when they land in Atlanta?"

"Because that will kill the chance of tracking her to who we really need to get to shut this ring down."

"You're right." Bri would be back in the States, but they needed to aim higher than Tawnya to keep Bri safe afterward.

"While she's separated from Tawnya, they'll plant a tracker in her suitcase and pass along a message not to go with Tawnya."

"There's a chance they'll miss her. You need to let me pose as the agent."

"Not a chance. I've already told you that. Bri might react to spotting you, or Tawnya could know what you look like and make the connection. Either blows this operation."

"I can wear glasses and put on some fake facial hair, they'll never—"

"No! We need you available to impersonate Malloy if Tawnya calls." Clara shut him down. "HSI will have their pictures and know what flight they're on. They can handle this."

Even though he'd spent years following orders, giving up control in this situation ranked high on his list of orders he most wanted to disobey.

"There's more. Apparently, she doesn't want to risk Bri changing her mind or getting away now that she finally agreed because Tawnya texted she changed their flight reservation. Since I'd already contacted HSI, they got through security and made the flight that left around seven p.m. their time. They'll be in Raleigh tomorrow afternoon."

"Tomorrow? Okay. That's—that's good. But—"

"I've alerted HSI to the change. We need to scramble to get things in place. I'll let you know more tomorrow. We're almost there. There's nothing else we can do tonight. I'm going to get some sleep. You should too."

Sleep? Right. Linc stared at his phone after Clara ended the call.

"Are you okay?" Kendra asked softly.

"Her being on her way back home is what we want."

"Are you going to be able to sleep?"

She could already read him almost as well as his teammates could. He stared at the ceiling and sighed. "No guarantees." He had to plan for contingencies of what could go wrong. That meant refocusing rather than picking up where he'd been with Kendra. "I need to go for a run. I might be awhile. Do you want me to go ahead and move Jalen back out here?"

"Don't risk waking him. We can share the bed."

"Now you're making me jealous." He winked as he retrieved his workout clothes from his bag.

"It's a king-size bed. There's room for two and a half if you want instead of sleeping on the couch. I'd hate for your neck to get stiff again."

"Maybe I'll do that." Obviously, they wouldn't fool around with Jalen in the bed. After Bri was home, he and Kendra could see where things went.

In the darkness, he ran hard the first mile through Dev's neighborhood, burning off anger, frustration, and too much energy he needed to conserve. Once he slowed his pace, he worked through potential scenarios that could go down and put Bri at risk.

Then it hit him. If Tawnya called or tried to video chat when they arrived, she expected Malloy to be at the airport with Jalen. Maybe not *inside* the airport, but in a parking lot or deck. It wasn't in the capacity he wanted, but he *did* have to be at the airport.

If he were there, he could stake out Tawnya's car. There was no way he would let Bri leave with her. Except he needed to know the make, model, and license plate to find it. Clara had to have that information. Would she tell him? He could place a tracker on the vehicle, so if something went wrong with tagging Bri's suitcase authorities wouldn't lose her.

He needed to make sure Clara and HSI operated with the best information and action plan. Stopping, he pulled out his phone and sent a text message to Clara, then resumed his run, hoping he'd hear back from her tonight.

After roughly half an hour, he returned to the house, drenched from running in the North Carolina humidity. Kendra had left the light over the stove on, but the rest of the house was dark. However, she'd also left the bedroom door ajar.

After downing a glass of water, he went to the guest bathroom and turned on the shower.

As he stripped off his sweaty clothes, he thought about how he could help Kendra work through her past and have confidence for a future relationship. Though it sucked for him, he'd overheard her and Clara at Malloy's house earlier. He needed to be upfront with her that his long-term plans did not include marriage and family—even if spending so much time with her these past few days had him thinking beyond the short-term.

He couldn't blame her for wanting more. Hell, he did too. Years ago, he'd accepted that wasn't his lot in life. While he would kill to protect Jalen, he didn't date women with kids.

He didn't want to risk being responsible for breaking their hearts. A relationship or marriage ending didn't always mean problems like in his mother's life, though, with his family history, he didn't want to take chances. With what Kendra shared about her aunt killing her husband, she'd likely understand that.

He stepped under the warm spray. As he washed, he imagined it was Kendra's hand rather than his gliding up and down his stiff cock. Better to self-gratify than lay in bed thinking about Kendra and things that we're not happening tonight—or maybe ever.

He turned the water to cold to finish off the shower. As he toweled off, he debated her offer to sleep in the bed. Leaving the door open came across as an invitation, which, if he didn't accept it, could send the wrong message or been seen as rejection. Though she deserved someone who could give her the life she wanted. Besides, her entire family would have serious concerns about her even dating a man who served in the military, especially since movies and television loved to portray guys in the Special Ops community as unhinged—or worse.

Since his only pair of gym shorts were damp from the run, he dressed in clean boxers and pulled on a T-shirt. He turned off the light in the kitchen and let his eyes adjust to the dark before opening the bedroom door wider.

"Was the run helpful?" Kendra let him know she was awake.

"Yeah." He entered the room. "I texted Clara. Hopefully, I'll hear back in the morning."

Kendra rolled to her side and edged closer to where Jalen slept on the side of the bed. She even lifted the sheet.

He lay on his side. In the faint light, he made out her face inches from his. Her smile grew.

"What?" he asked.

"I was just thinking how we'd answer if someone were to ask how we met. I could say we met through Bri, though I'd leave out the 'I was her social worker' part and not mention a drug smuggling operation as a matchmaker."

He gave a gruff chuckle, and Jalen stirred. He liked how she'd respected Bri's privacy, even if she wouldn't tell her family, or even her friends, if they went out a few times. His team would know how they met, not that he'd introduce her to them. Over the years, there'd only been two women he'd been with long enough to meet his team family. "I know you've picked up on what I do, but it's important that you not share that—with anyone."

"I am aware and understand."

"Thanks." For now, there was no harm in rolling with the fantasy of meeting each other's friends. "I can use the 'It's classified.' response or just stare at them without answering." He had that down pat.

He couldn't resist reaching to run the back of his fingers across the silky skin of her cheek before kissing her—sweet, relatively chaste kisses given the situation, but the kind that burrowed beneath his armor.

The way she made him feel respected and of worth went deeper than physical attraction and needs. He shouldn't let it go to his head. In addition to looking for the good in people, she might be swayed, viewing him as Jalen's and her protector the past few days.

She had one arm curled under her head. He took hold of her free hand and kissed her forehead. Breathing in a light powder scent, he closed his eyes, trusting that Kendra and Clara were right, and that Bri would be home safely tomorrow.

EIGHTEEN

When he woke in bed next to Kendra, Linc only wanted one thing more than to stay right there. What he most wanted motivated him to ease out from under the covers without waking her or Jalen. Before he even dressed, he checked his phone. No message from Clara yet, but it wasn't even seven a.m. Waiting would make this a long day.

He had breakfast underway when Jalen wandered into the kitchen.

"I have school today?" He climbed onto the bar stool and started spinning in circles.

"Not today. It's an Uncle-Linc's-in-town holiday." As much as he banked on Bri being home today, he didn't want to get Jalen's hopes up. "We'll go see Grams at the hospital later. First, we're having breakfast—with *orange rolls*."

Jalen stopped spinning, his mouth and eyes opened wide. "They're my favorite!"

"I know." Bri's too. Hopefully, she'd get to have leftovers tomorrow. "We'll also have bacon and eggs."

"*Cheesy* eggs."

Linc laughed. Could this kid be any cuter? It would suck to have his nephew's life turned upside down.

Kendra joined them a few minutes later. She'd already dressed and had on a touch of makeup.

"Water in the pot is hot if you want tea."

"You're spoiling me." She added water and a tea bag to the mug he'd set out, then came to his side and laid a hand on the small of his back. "What can I do to help?"

He leaned in and kissed her. "That's a start." It was hard to tell if she blushed, but her bashful smile was a nice way to start the morning.

His phone finally rang as he pulled out his semi-crisp bacon from the skillet. "Did you get my message about finding Tawnya's car at the airport?" he asked Clara.

"Yes, we were already on that. I wanted to see if it would be okay for me to come by and fill you in on the plan for today."

"Of course. We're about to eat breakfast."

"I'll be there in less than ten minutes. I haven't eaten yet because I've been working on this case," she added.

Kendra shook her head. Laughing she grabbed more eggs. She cooked Jalen's eggs and added cheese.

By the time Clara arrived, Jalen had finished his food, and Linc had set him up with the iPad and noise-cancelling headphones so they could discuss the plan without him picking up on their conversation.

Clara devoured an orange roll and a piece of bacon before she sat. "It looks like Malloy will survive. He's conscious, and we have him under guard. The hospital staff have all been informed not to let him have access to any telephones or computers."

"Has he given any information?"

"We haven't questioned him or pressed charges yet

because he may ask for a lawyer. If he does, whomever they work for will get word. We want to get Bri back safely first."

"Smart," he concurred. Any big crime organization would have lawyers who'd report back that the police had Malloy. That would put Bri in even more danger.

Kendra slid a plate of eggs and bacon to Clara.

"HSI located Tawnya's vehicle. They've got a long-range tracker on it, and they'll have someone in the lot eyeballing it. They will not let Bri get in the vehicle with her," Clara assured him. "You're right about needing to be at the airport, along with Jalen. And it's best if Kendra comes too. However, while you can use the app to impersonate Malloy over the phone, you can't pass in person. HSI has an agent who's about the right size and coloring. He'll drive Malloy's van and get Jalen out if necessary. In addition to planting the tracker and letting Bri know not to go with Tawnya, their agent will slip Bri a button cam so we can see and hear what's going on after she gets through security. That'll help us know how to react."

"I'm impressed with your planning for contingencies," Linc stated.

"Glad to hear you approve. HSI tends to be the best of the best at what *they* do." Clara winked at him. "When you retire from the military, maybe you'll consider Homeland Security as an option. You'd make an excellent police officer, though here might be a little tame for you."

"I've got another eight years left before I'd consider retiring." He decided to put that on the table in case she intended that as a hint of a way to get her family's approval.

"We've got a couple of hours, but I'd like to get out to the airport early to get an overview of the layout and where we need to be. Hopefully, their last flight is on time, but you'll want to bring some things to keep Jalen occupied."

"I can help with that," Kendra offered.

"I sent Bri's driver's license and passport pictures to HSI, but forward me any recent pictures you have, and I'll pass them along. I'll be back at noon. The van only has the driver and passenger seats, so we'll need to take another car. Thanks for the food," she said to Kendra.

"Thank him. He did most of it."

"He cooks too? What's your MOS?"

"His what?" Kendra eyed Clara like she'd said something dirty.

"Military occupational specialty," Linc explained. "Engineer and anything to do with computers."

"Those are opposite ends of the spectrum," Clara commented.

"What can I say? I'm well-rounded." He shrugged.

"I bet you are." Clara grinned. "Maybe we can double date so Derrick can meet you. We can go to the shooting range and then to dinner."

The shooting range wasn't exactly what he had in mind for a date with Kendra, but if he passed muster with her cousin, that wouldn't be bad. "I've got a while left on this deployment, but after that, sure."

LINC TOOK Jalen to the playground and made him run around for an hour to expend some energy, though it didn't guarantee he would nap later.

"I packed some snacks and his backpack with his things, so he won't have to come back here. I also downloaded a couple of episodes of his favorite shows onto my tablet to keep him from getting too bored," Kendra told Linc after they returned.

That she'd also cleaned up the kitchen and bathrooms,

washed sheets, and had them in the dryer was the kind of optimism Linc needed. "I haven't said anything about Bri coming home today," he told her. "If I did, he'd ask a million times how much longer. And I don't want him disappointed if there's a glitch."

Linc went back to the garage and moved the booster seat back into his car. Then he retrieved the goldfish crackers from Dev's seat and floor. He'd add a car wash and tank of gas to the list of things he owed Dev. For two guys with opposite backgrounds, they'd clicked from Dev's first week joining the Bad Karma team. Linc and the rest of the team hadn't known then that Dev came from a *very* wealthy family. But he worked as hard as any guy on the team. Smart as hell and, being an adrenaline junkie, up to any challenge.

This team was the best Linc had ever worked with due largely to Chief Lundgren's leadership. Linc could lose his spot if he had to stay here for Bri and Jalen for an extended period. Being transferred to another team wasn't the *worst* thing that could happen, but it would suck because this was more than a team—they were his family, not by blood, but by choice.

He went inside the house and dumped the crackers into the trash. Since he wouldn't leave for a couple more days, he'd have time to come back and clean out the fridge, take out the trash, and do whatever else needed to be done later.

Clara knocked on the door a few minutes before noon. "I got word their flight landed in Atlanta. They have about a three-hour layover. An undercover HSI officer is keeping an eye on them to make sure there's no handoff there. We're ready to roll."

Linc picked up Jalen's camouflage backpack. "J-man, we're going for a ride."

"Back to Beckham's house?"

"Not today. But maybe later this week, we can go to the park."

Before getting to the airport outside Raleigh, an airliner passed low over them on the highway.

"Are we here to get Mommy?" Jalen strained against the seatbelt holding him in his booster seat to peer at the plane.

Linc knew better than to lie. Jalen might have some learning issues, but there was no doubt in Linc's mind that this kid was smart. "We are. But her flight doesn't get in for a while. Miss Clara and I have to go to the airport, and you're going to stay with Miss Kendra. Then we're going to surprise Mommy. I need you to be good and not ask how much longer every five minutes."

Clara turned into the cell phone lot and motioned for Linc to pull alongside her. Kendra lowered the window.

"I'm not sure how long this will be. Linc, you can ride with me, and Kendra can take Jalen somewhere for lunch."

"Good idea," Linc agreed.

"Park in the central lot between the terminals when you get back," Clara instructed Kendra.

He got out of the car to switch places. As they met at the front of the car, he handed Kendra his keys and pulled out his wallet. "Let me give you money for lunch."

"Not necessary." She pressed a kiss to his cheek. "I'll put it on your tab." She gave a playful wink and smile before getting in the driver's seat and closing the door.

Linc climbed into the passenger seat of the van. Clara's smug smile made him keenly aware she had been watching them.

"So, how much sway does Grandma Ruby have?"

"You mean when it comes to her feelings about family members getting involved with military men? You know that saying, *she's a force to be reckoned with*?"

That didn't sound good.

"You know ordnance. Sometimes you diffuse the bomb. Other times you do your best to dodge them." She drove into the central lot. "Kendra's a people pleaser, but she's realizing it's time to make *herself* happy."

"What type of guys does she date?"

"Since I've been with Derrick, the only one I've met is Marcus. And I wouldn't say he was her type."

"Why's that?"

"He was—boring. Very career and money focused."

"What kind of work did he do?"

"He's an attorney. Personally, I think he liked showing Kendra off to his law partners since she was younger and, frankly, out of his league."

She might be out of Linc's league, too, though she didn't make him feel that way.

"You'll need to leave your weapon in the van. *You* aren't allowed to carry firearms into the airport."

"I've got my Marshal credentials."

"You're not here as a Marshal. It's a courtesy they're letting either of us be involved."

He removed his weapon from its holster and placed it in the glove box, which Clara then locked.

She carried a bag with her as they walked to the terminal.

"How'd they meet?" Linc probed further.

"He represented a family in an adoption case, and they worked together. She accepted his dinner invite because he went the extra mile for the family. Then, he invited her to a children's charity event fundraiser. The kind of thing she wouldn't say no to. He was high bidder on several items in the silent auction. Since she was his date, he invited her to join him at one of the finer restaurants in Fayetteville. He also won the auction for a week's stay at someone's timeshare in Cancun, which I think he strategically bid on."

"Because he invited her to go with him?"

"He waited until they'd been going out longer, but yes. He claimed he bid on it because she'd commented on how beautiful it looked, and he thought it would be a great way to celebrate his fortieth birthday. I think she felt pressured to go. Not only by Marcus, but he'd won Grandma Ruby over, and she convinced Kendra that his wanting to take her on a luxurious trip showed how committed he was."

It sounded manipulative to Linc, though it could be a bit of jealousy. They entered Terminal Two, and Clara texted to inform HSI they were there.

"Marcus started talking about marriage. She wants to get married, but she wants kids, and, at his age. he doesn't. So, she ended things. Expensive houses, cars, and trips aren't what appeals to Kendra. Seeing how you are with Jalen? Now that's another story."

Clara clearly meant it as a compliment. However, as much as he wanted to date Kendra, maybe he shouldn't waste her time. He couldn't give her the things she wanted either. It'd be better to put his cards on the table rather than wait. Maybe then it wouldn't feel like she rejected him.

A man wearing plain clothes approached. "Detective Lowe?"

"Yes, and this is Staff Sergeant Lincoln Porter. He's been assisting us since learning his sister was being held and forced to be a courier."

"I'm Officer Harkness. I'm sorry she's going through this. However, it looks like she could be one of the lucky ones. Follow me."

Lucky? Linc hoped so.

Harkness swiped his badge at an unmarked door,

punched in the keypad code, then led them to a private security screening area. Upon producing her credentials, Clara passed her weapon through. It was probably best that Linc didn't have the temptation of being armed. Besides, he didn't need a firearm to restrain Tawnya.

Inside a small conference room, Harkness introduced them to the other HSI officers detailed to this mission.

"Officer Garcia will pull your sister for secondary inspection." He pointed at the petite officer who looked like a high school student.

"The plan was to pass your sister a button camera with a mic. However, that's not going to work. Our officers in Atlanta took this." Garcia slid them a picture of Bri pulling a suitcase. "There are no buttons on her top. Fahey might well be watching and notice her putting on or suddenly wearing a necklace."

"What are your other options?" Linc asked. The best of the best would have a plan B and C.

"We don't want to attach anything to the suitcase that might get noticed. And since they took her phone, I don't want to take the chance of Fahey seeing me slip Miss Porter a phone, especially when we can't get video. Besides, the audio from inside her big purse is questionable. The new plan is for me to give her this camera pen to clip to the edge of her purse. We probably won't get a great video of Tawnya's face to get a read on her, but the audio should be good."

"I'll keep an eye on Fahey to see if she's watching Garcia search Ms. Porter's bag and how she reacts," Patton, the plainclothes female officer who looked like a middle-aged tourist, said. "Fahey could panic and leave rather than risk getting caught. Though Garcia here doesn't usually come across as threatening."

"I love being underestimated by these kinds of people," Garcia gave a big smile.

Linc nodded, breathing easier.

"Ms. Fahey doesn't know that we've recovered Miss Porter's grandmother or that her partner, Malloy, was shot during the rescue and is under guard in the hospital," Clara informed the HSI officers. "We cloned his phone, and Staff Sergeant Porter created filters which have worked to make Fahey think she's been communicating with Malloy and that he managed to abduct Miss Porter's son. The sergeant needs to be looped in to best handle the call to facilitate trading Miss Porter's son for the suitcase with the drugs."

"I created a filter to mask my appearance so I would look like him. Fortunately, it's been voice calls," Linc explained.

"How do you know what he sounds like?" Garcia asked.

"We got lucky there because the Fayetteville PD had video from an interrogation we could use," Clara answered.

"Do you have to type in what you want to say? Cuz that delay could be a giveaway," Costa, the agent about the same build and who should pass for Malloy from a distance, sounded intrigued.

"AI has gotten very advanced. With the program running, it alters *any* voice to sound like him in real-time. Though you still have to be careful in what you say, " Linc explained. "Word choices. Pronunciation. Talking too much or giving the wrong answer."

"It's scary," Garcia said. "Someone claiming to be my cousin called my grandmother saying his wallet had been stolen on a trip, and he needed her to wire him money. He knew my cousin's name, and she said it sounded like him. Fortunately, my grandmother was suspicious because we'd warned her about all these scams. She asked a question that he answered wrong."

"That's exactly why we want to limit the interaction as much as possible," Linc added.

"Not a problem," Officer Harkness assured them. "And you brought her son?"

"His social worker is with us as well." Clara didn't go into details about their relationship. "She took him to get lunch while we met with you. They'll be back shortly."

"I guess we'll put all four of you in the van with Officer Costa," Harkness said.

"It's going to be crowded in that van. I'm happy to help with surveillance," Clara suggested.

"I won't turn down another pair of eyes when we're devoting most of our resources to this case," Harkness agreed.

Clara handed Costa the bag she'd brought in. "This is one of Malloy's shirts and the ball cap he wore when he abducted Mrs. Feldman. If you keep enough distance, you should be able to pass for Malloy."

"I hope so. I shaved for this." Costa ran a hand over his face.

"He's been needing to shave that porn star mustache for months now." Garcia's ribbing reminded Linc of his team.

"Let's go do a walk-through." Harkess led them to the door. "Where they'll come in. Where we'll take Miss Porter for the inspection. Then, you and Costa can plan possible exit scenarios. Officer Patton will proceed to the parking garage, watching for Fahey. I'll be in a separate chase vehicle, and we'll tail her to the drop off. Stopping drugs coming into the States is an everyday thing for us. This might not be a huge haul, but that they kidnapped an innocent elderly woman and went after a kid? This crew and whoever they're working for need to go down."

The other three HSI officers wore what Linc would call their *mission-go* faces. Together, they had this.

NINETEEN

After walking through the terminal and the arrivals area, Clara handed Costa the van's key fob and returned to the HSI office with Harkness. Costa and Linc remained in the arrivals area, watching the flow of traffic and plotting placements before Costa relayed information about the operation to the personnel directing traffic.

Once Kendra texted that they were back and parked in the central lot near the van, they headed there. Linc walked Costa to Malloy's van and then met Kendra at his car.

"Where's Mommy?" Jalen asked the moment Linc slid into the passenger seat.

"Her plane's landing soon. We'll hang out here until it's time to meet her."

"O-kay," Jalen drew the word out. The last thing Linc wanted was to give him a reason to be disappointed.

"Something smells good. Besides you." He leaned closer to Kendra.

"I brought you a burrito and drink." She reached into the backseat and produced a bag.

The way he'd grown up, a woman providing him food

earned his loyalty, especially that he hadn't asked her to bring him something. "Thanks."

"Coms check," Harkness requested and waited for everyone to check in. "Their plane's at the gate, and the doors are open."

Linc's adrenaline flowed. "Hey, J-man. I need you to use these." He handed back the pair of headphones.

As he finished his burrito, he watched the clock numbers change over the next twelve minutes of radio silence. Waiting was always the hard part.

That Jalen hadn't asked him how much longer for at least five minutes made Linc open the mirror on the visor. Peering behind him, he chuckled at Jalen's closed eyes and open mouth. His head rested against the side of the booster seat as the tablet continued to play his show.

"It always amazes me how kids can sleep in some of the most uncomfortable positions." Kendra placed her hand over Linc's and gazed at Jalen. She wore a serene smile that reminded him of what Clara had said Kendra wanted for her future. Only now wasn't the time to have that discussion. For now, he was content to sit and absorb her reassuring presence.

"I have eyes on the targets now," Garcia reported.

Linc listened to her request passports from several travelers.

"How long were you in Mexico?" Garcia asked another passenger.

"Not quite a week."

Hearing Bri's voice felt like making it through a violent storm—only the calm could be the eye of a hurricane if they didn't take down the high-level players running this operation.

"Was your trip for work or vacation?"

"Vacation."

"It doesn't look like you got much sun," Garcia commented.

"I caught something. I spent most of the week in the hotel room."

"I'm sorry to hear that. Come with me for a bag check."

"Why?"

The way Bri's voice shot up in pitch, Linc didn't need to see her face to know she was panicking.

"Just a routine inspection. Are you traveling alone?" Garcia asked.

"No. I went with a, uh, a friend."

"Is he or she still with you?"

"She was with me until you pulled me over here. I think she's waiting for me since she's my ride."

"This will just take a few minutes. Place your bag up here. Did you have any checked bags?"

"No, just this one."

"Target subject is waiting and watching target two with Garcia near the phone store," Patton spoke over Garcia. "And she looks nervous."

"They both do," Clara added.

The cloned burner of Malloy's phone rang. Linc tapped his earpiece. "Fahey is calling me," he reported in before he answered the call. "Yeah." He exited the car to prevent the chance of Jalen waking up and calling him by name.

"We may have a problem," Tawnya spoke lowly and rapidly.

"What now?"

"Security pulled her. They are going through her bag now."

"She won't say anything when we've got her kid." Linc tried to keep Tawnya from panicking.

"Maybe not, but I can't afford to have my name flagged in the system."

Linc grunted. "For sure." That was not going to be her biggest problem. "Give it a minute."

"If they bring over a dog or take her for secondary inspection, I'll need to make a fast exit. Are you close by?"

"I'm close." If Tawnya would shut up, he could hear Garcia and Bri.

"Your brother got your message, and we know what you're being forced to do," Garcia spoke reassuringly.

"You do?" Bri squeaked.

"Authorities raided the house where Ms. Fahey's partner held your grandmother. She's all right."

"What about my son? They had him and my friend."

"They're fine. They never found your son."

"They did. I saw a video," Bri insisted.

"Keep looking at *me*. She's watching us. Relax and smile. Police made that video of him with your social worker," Garcia said. "We're going to let you through. Let Fahey take the suitcase, but under no circumstances are you to get in the vehicle with her. Do you understand?"

"I'm telling you, this one's been a total pain in the ass this whole time," Tawnya grumbled. "She must be freaking the hell out. She's packing up her suitcase, and the agent is inspecting her purse. They're letting her go, but this feels off."

Invisible spiders swarmed all over Linc's body. "This might be this agent's first day on the job and our lucky day."

"You might be right. The agent doesn't look old enough to drive. She's got the suitcase and coming this way. I'll see what she says." Tawnya ended the call in time for him to make out Garcia's voice through his earpiece.

"I didn't tell her I planted a tracker in the suitcase or

about the pen mic. I was afraid she might give it away as nervous as she was."

"Good call. Tawnya's already suspicious," Linc said. It was ironic that the police were successfully keeping Bri in the dark about what they'd hidden in the suitcase, whereas she'd figured out Tawnya's plan. *That's karma for you, Tawnya.*

"What happened?" Tawnya's voice came through the pen mic with only a little distortion.

"She said it was a routine bag check," Bri answered.

"What did you tell her?" Tawnya continued her interrogation.

"They're moving toward the exit," Officer Patton reported.

"I just answered her questions. I guess she decided I didn't fit their profile because of the length of stay and because I bought my own ticket in advance. You're smart there." Bri didn't make it sound like a compliment.

Tawnya snorted.

"I've done my part and got your precious drugs through security. Now, I want my son, or I walk back to that nice agent and tell her the truth."

"You do that, and you may never see your son again."

"If you hurt him, you'll wish we never met."

Tawnya gave an ominous, hollow laugh. "Don't threaten me. And don't even think about calling the police. My people know where to find you."

"I just want my son and my grandmother and to never see you again."

"We've got your son outside."

"And my grandmother?"

"*After* we deliver the suitcase."

A text popped up on the cloned phone.

> Bring the boy. We'll be at zone five

> Leaving the parking deck now

Linc texted back.

"Wait here until I contact you," he said to Kendra before getting out and unbuckling a groggy Jalen.

"Are we going to see Mommy now?"

"We are. We're going to ride in this van." He opened the sliding door, set Jalen inside, and then climbed in.

His team usually brainstormed their missions, with Chief Lundgren having the final say. Only they weren't here. They'd faced dozens of dangerous missions where they couldn't control factors.

He should have thought this through better. Make Bri come to the van and have Costa and Malloy shove her in. But if Fahey saw Costa, that could tank things as much as Jalen divulging Linc was here.

What if they messed this up, and Tawnya didn't lead them to her bosses? Would they target Bri? Even Jalen or Kendra?

This had to work.

Linc stayed low and out of sight as Costa entered the arrivals area.

"I see them. Passing them now." Costa navigated around cars stopped in the middle of the lane to pick up passengers, parked at the curb, and then climbed into the back of the van.

"He's going to get you out," Linc told Jalen. "When you see Mommy, I want you to run to her and give her hugs and kisses."

"Big hugs!"

Costa held onto Jalen as they exited the van, and Linc got into position to watch out the dark tinted back window.

"Jalen!" Bri's cry came through Linc's earpiece. Jalen either heard or spotted Bri because he took off running.

Linc's vision blurred as Bri abandoned the suitcase and dashed to scoop Jalen into her arms. The sound of noisy kisses warmed his heart.

"I missed you, Mommy."

"I've missed you so much, baby." Bri's voice broke, and she choked on a sob.

Costa didn't waste any time getting back in the van.

"Aww, isn't this sweet?" Tawnya said in that nasally tone that grated on Linc's nerves. She gripped a suitcase handle in each hand. "Let's get out of here."

"I'm not going anywhere with you." Bri went into bitch mode.

"Are you going to walk to my house from here?"

"I'll get a taxi or borrow a phone to call a friend. A *real* friend. Because I'm sure as hell not putting my son in the car with you."

"What about your things?"

Linc couldn't determine if she meant Bri's belongings in the suitcase or Regina and Kendra.

"Nothing in there means anything to me. Just take your crap and go. But if you or your kidnapper friend lay a hand on me or my son, I'm going to scream so loud that every cop in this area is coming down on you. We are done."

"What about your grandma and the social worker?"

"Make the delivery and let them go, and you won't have to worry about me."

"We've got to move." Costa edged into the line of cars exiting the airport.

Linc slid into the passenger seat and watched out the side-view mirror as Tawnya raised a hand as if signaling them.

When Costa kept going, she released her grip on her suitcase and pulled out her phone.

Linc answered the call. "What's going on?" he played dumb.

"She's not cooperating on coming with me. Where are you going?"

"Traffic cop was coming. You got the suitcase?"

"Yeah, but—"

"But nothin'. Get out of there. I'm not risking sticking around. Make the delivery. Pack up and get out of town—and the state."

"This is worse than Nashville."

Costa smacked the phone from Linc's hand and laid on the horn. "Asshole driver," he muttered loudly for no apparent reason. He waved Linc off when he reached for the phone.

"I can't hear you," Costa spoke loudly. "Some asshole about sideswiped me. Can't reach my phone. Talk to you later."

Once the screen went black, Linc picked up the phone and checked that the call had ended.

"Her mentioning another city smelled like it could be a trap to verify she was talking to Malloy. Didn't want to risk it."

"Smart move," Linc concurred.

"You said the program would mimic *anyone's* voice. I took you at your word." He turned left and circled back toward arrivals.

"I'm tailing our subject to the parking deck," Patton reported.

The loud smack of kisses coming through his earpiece allowed Linc to draw in his first full breath in days. Bri was home. She was safe.

"Are you all right, sweetie?" Bri asked. "I'm sorry. So sorry."

"I wanna go home wif you, Mommy," Jalen said.

"Me too. I need to figure that out."

"Let me know when we're clear to approach Bri before she gets in a taxi," Clara requested.

"Fahey's at the elevator. You're good to go," Patton said a minute later.

"Excuse me, Miss Porter. I'm Detective Lowe."

"Detective? I don't have any drugs on me. I swear. They hid them in a suitcase, and—"

"We know. And that you were forced to bring them. We got the message you left on your grandmother's phone."

"Is my grandmother she really safe?"

"She was dehydrated and shaken up, so they kept her in the hospital overnight, but she'll be fine."

"Thank God. And Kendra Andrews? She's my—"

"Kendra's fine. They didn't get her or Jalen."

"But I saw video of them."

"We filmed them so you'd cooperate to get you out of Mexico. Tawnya's partner never found them," Clara assured her.

"I thought—" Bri choked on a sob.

As he listened, Linc's gut twisted into tight knots. Had Bri not seen Kendra wearing his necklace and gotten the message? His plan hadn't worked, and he'd added to her stress with her thinking Jalen was in danger. As Costa entered the arrivals area again, Linc scanned the passengers, looking for Bri. When Costa pulled to the curb, Linc opened his door and exited before the van came to a complete stop.

"Uncle Linc!" Jalen called and waved an arm.

Bri spun, her mouth dropping open just before Linc

reached her. "You're here?" Her voice wobbled. He wrapped his arms around her and Jalen, and she clung to him. "How'd you know?"

He loosened his hold on her slightly. "I got your message. When I couldn't reach you, I got worried and took emergency family leave."

"I can't believe you're here." She raised her face and stared at him with damp eyes.

"Your brother filing a missing person's report for Mrs. Feldman aided in our investigation," Clara said. "He wanted to fly down to Mexico to find you himself."

"I would have gone if I'd had any idea where to find you." He brushed away her tears with his thumb.

"I was going to tell you when I called. But Tawnya—" Bri's eyes widened, and her head jerked toward the parking deck. "You need to stop Tawnya."

"Two Homeland Security officers are tailing her to the delivery," Clara assured her. "We'll get her, and, hopefully, the people she works for."

"Good." Bri exhaled, then took another deep breath. "Before I could tell you what was happening, Tawyna came in, and I had to hang up. I was going to call you back because I knew you'd know what I should do. I pretended I didn't know they'd switched the suitcase she'd lent me with an identical one, but she overheard enough to know I'd figured out their plan. When we went to the pool, she not so *accidentally* knocked me into the water while I had my phone, so it died."

"You were smart to get hold of hers to call," Linc said.

"I called Grams to warn her, but Tawnya caught me. It went downhill from there. I didn't know if I'd even see you again." She kissed Jalen who played with the lock of her coppery brown hair that had escaped her hair clip.

"If it weren't for your brother, we might not have had any

idea what was going on or how to get you back here," Clara said. "I will need to get your statement, but that can wait until tomorrow. I imagine you need some rest, and it would be better to make sure we get the details straight. And you'd probably like some time with your son and to check on your grandmother."

"Yes. Thank you. Thank you. I can't believe this nightmare is finally over." Her body sagged into Linc's.

He dialed Kendra.

"Is everything all right?" she immediately asked.

"Went down without a hitch. You can pick us up in zone five."

"Thank goodness. See you in a minute."

"I'll let you know how things wrap up." Costa returned the van keys to Clara. "Trade you."

Linc removed the camera pen attached to the top of Bri's purse, removed his earpiece, and handed them to Costa.

"What's that?" Bri pointed to the pen.

"A recording device, so we could listen in. Officer Garcia clipped it on when she checked your purse. And she planted a GPS tracker in your suitcase to make sure we don't lose it or Fahey and can locate who she's taking the drugs to," Costa answered.

"You don't know how relieved I am that you figured this out and are here."

Kendra parked Linc's car at the curb and got out. She rushed to Bri, and the two embraced.

"I'm so, so sorry. I don't know how you got dragged into this."

"The school called me when your grandmother didn't pick Jalen up, and they couldn't get hold of her or Linc. Fortunately, your brother arrived and got my message. He's been taking excellent care of Jalen, hasn't he?" She rubbed the boy's back.

"Uh-huh!" Jalen nodded emphatically. "Uncle Linc built me a blanket fort. He made me pancakes and cheesy eggs. And I have a new friend, Beckham."

They'd done it—together. "Kendra was a big help with him, and if she hadn't called her cousin, Detective Lowe here, to make searching for Regina and her car a priority, we might not have found her."

"We make a good team," Clara said. "I'll even put in a good word for you with Ruby."

"For a job with the police?" Bri asked wide-eyed.

"No. I'll explain later," Linc said with a shake of his head.

"I was stupid to go to Mexico with a drug smuggler I thought was my friend. Will this affect my custody?" Tears brimmed in Bri's eyes, and she hugged Jalen tighter to her side.

"No. You haven't been my client for well over a year now. I don't need to report any of this. Besides, you didn't do anything wrong," Kendra assured Bri.

"She's right. They took advantage of you," Clara chimed in. "We have reason to believe they've run the same scenario out of different cities, and they know who to target and what works to convince you. There's a third partner who's down in Mexico right now. Authorities there are keeping an eye on him and hoping to discover their supplier to take down that arm of the organization."

"I can't believe they'd pay for airfare and a week at a luxury hotel just to smuggle a few pounds of drugs into the States."

"There's a pretty steep profit margin," Clara stated. "Depending on the type of drugs, they can cover that cost ten to twenty times over. If someone doesn't know they're carrying, there's a much higher probability of getting through because they won't act suspicious and draw HSI's attention. Plus, they're not paying the carrier a fee, so it's a trade-off."

Bri shivered. "I don't even want to think about what happened if someone else figured it out or got caught. Tawnya kept threatening to turn me over to some woman, Inez, who, um . . ." She cut her gaze to Jalen and didn't finish.

"We know. That's why we made the video and let Tawnya think they had Jalen, to get you to agree. We alerted authorities there so they'd let you through security," Clara explained.

"Didn't you see Kendra wearing my necklace in the video?" Linc pulled out the cord with his half-heart.

"No. As soon as I saw Jalen, I started crying. Everything was blurry."

"I thought you'd see the necklace and know I was here. Kendra was trying to tell you that we knew, and you'd be okay."

Bri shook her head. "I missed that. When I thought they had Jalen, agreeing to smuggle the suitcase was my only option. Don't tell Grams I wouldn't agree when I knew they had her."

"I'm sure she would understand, but mums the word." He gave her a reassuring squeeze.

"Do you want to ride back to Fayetteville with me?" Clara asked Kendra. "If they go to the hospital, they'll probably take Mrs. Feldman home."

"Good idea." Kendra made eye contact with Linc as she placed his car keys in his hand.

"I'll touch base with you later." He refrained from kissing her in front of his sister for now. He didn't want to get into details about a romantic relationship developing while trying to find and rescue both her and Regina.

"Bye, Jalen. I'll see you again soon." Kendra touched Jalen's back, her fingers lingering there.

"Let's take your mommy home, J-man." Linc took Jalen from Bri's arms.

By the end of the night, the people behind this smuggling operation could be under arrest, and Bri could put this nightmare behind her.

TWENTY

"Is it safe for me to go home now?" Kendra asked Clara as they exited the airport area.

"Should be. There's no upside to them coming after you now."

That's what she'd hoped to hear. "What about Bri?"

Clara sighed. "That depends on whether they arrest Tawnya and whoever she works for. Both Tawnya and Malloy face charges related to kidnapping as well as smuggling. Those are pretty hefty charges. We only need one to flip and agree to testify to take Bri out of the equation. If neither do, I can't rule out the possibility of her being targeted or facing retaliation."

"Damn," Kendra muttered.

"I know. She's not in trouble with us, but she's not home-free yet."

"Linc mentioned the possibility of her having to go into Witness Protection."

"It would have to be a pretty major case with someone way higher in the organization than Tawnya and Malloy to warrant putting them in Witness Protection."

Kendra breathed a bit easier hearing Clara's assessment. Not only would having a new identity be confusing for Jalen, but she couldn't imagine the toll it would have on Bri to lose Linc's support and for him to lose his only blood family.

Relief that Bri was home warred with the doubts that arose, wondering where things would go with Linc. She understood Bri would be his focus until he left to finish his deployment. How would things change then? Would they be able to message and video chat to move things forward?

When they arrived at her apartment, Kendra dug her keys out of her purse.

"I'm going to check your place, just to be safe." Clara shut off the engine. "I'll get the surveillance cameras tomorrow. They might help you sleep better tonight."

"Thanks for putting in overtime on this."

"Anything for family. Besides, it was one of the more exciting cases I've worked." She drew her weapon and entered first.

Exciting wasn't the word Kendra would use to describe the past few days. And though accustomed to facing danger, Linc probably hadn't considered this case 'exciting.' Not with how personal it had been. However, Bri's reaction when she thought Clara was recruiting Linc for the police department showed that she knew her brother was committed to his military service and team. Fear of her family's disapproval and what happened with her aunt was why she'd listened to Grandma Ruby's warnings about dating a guy in the military. But the rest of her family wouldn't excommunicate her, not if they gave Linc a chance.

Clara checked all the rooms and closets. "All clear." She holstered her gun. Standing in front of the bookshelf, she picked up the framed picture of all the family from her and

Derrick's wedding. "Linc would fit in with our colorful mix. So would Bri and Jalen."

Kendra smiled as Clara set the frame back on the shelf next to the picture of Kendra in her graduation gown holding her master's in social work diploma, surrounded by her parents and three grandparents—another beautiful blend of color and heritages and love that stood up to prejudices to form the family who made her the woman she was today.

She locked the deadbolt when Clara left. The only sound was the hum of the air conditioner running. There'd be no banter about whose French fries tasted better. No building blanket forts. She might be safe, but these past few days with Linc and Jalen ramped up the longing for someone to spend her life with. A family of her own.

If Bri could overcome being sexually abused and succumbing to drugs to get her life on track and raise her son, Kendra could let go of the past and not let it control her. She also didn't have to settle for a guy because he checked the boxes her grandmother insisted were important. Marcus had strong ties to the community and a mid-six-figure income, but that wasn't a strong foundation on which to build a marriage. Not the kind of marriage and partnership she wanted.

Her undeniable attraction to Linc went deeper than his appealing appearance and physique. His loyalty to his family, his way of interacting with Jalen, and his understanding and support when she told him what had happened with Don were all values and character traits that she'd dreamed of in a spouse.

She checked emails and confirmed her appointments for tomorrow before making a salad and eating alone for the first time in several days. She sat at the secondhand kitchen table that she'd bought at Goodwill. It'd been covered with scratches, stains, and traces of marker before she and her mother sanded and painted it for an updated look and pop of color in the neutral palette of the apartment. Maybe it would be the center of family meals again one day.

What were Linc and Jalen doing now? She pictured Jalen's face and the wide-eyed smile that revealed a dimple in his cheek.

The memory of Linc's smile landing on her started a flutter in her stomach that went lower and changed to a pleasant pulsing. In a matter of days, Linc Porter had sent her world spinning in a new direction, and, damn, even the dizziness felt good.

An hour later, the knock at her front door made her jump. Her heart pounded even as she rationalized that there was no reason for Tawnya's associates to show up here now.

Peering through the peephole, her heart beat even harder. How did Linc even know where she lived? She backed away a step and took a deep breath, though that did nothing to slow her racing heart.

It was as if she'd summoned him.

She opened the door, fully aware of the smile on her face. "I didn't think I'd see you tonight."

"Sorry I didn't call before dropping in. I didn't want to wake you if you'd gone to bed." He entered her apartment and glanced around, taking it in.

"Not yet. I was headed that way."

Linc's unexpected visit made her glad she'd stayed up.

"Bri barely made it through eating the takeout we picked up before crashing."

"I imagine neither she nor Regina got much sleep the last few days."

"They'll all sleep well tonight. Clara called while Jalen and I were cleaning up and getting the food at Dev's place. She gave me your address so I could bring this over." He pulled out the box of English Breakfast tea from the grocery bag in his hand.

"You didn't need to come here to bring me tea bags." Though she didn't admit to the thrill of having him here.

"That wasn't the *only* reason." He handed her the bag with a sheepish grin.

She peeked inside. "Oh. How'd you know this was *my* underwear and not Dev's girlfriend's?"

"I was with you when you bought them. I saw the package and recognized the color."

Her face and neck heated, but she didn't say anything as she set the bag on the couch. She'd checked out that he bought boxer briefs too.

"I also wanted to tell you Clara said authorities arrested Tawnya *and* the high-level supplier she made the drop to. In addition to the drugs, they found firearms and cash in the house. It was a really good bust. She said Bri should only have to testify against Tawnya, which is a huge relief."

"That is good news." What he'd said about going to Dev's clicked in. "Is Jalen with you?"

"I took him back to Bri's. Regina's in Jalen's bed, and he's in with Bri. Since she's safe, I thought I'd sleep in my bed since she doesn't have a full-sized couch."

"Your house? Where there's no food?"

"I grabbed a protein bar. I've got to get up early to take Jalen to school for Bri. I'll get something while she and Regina give their statements to the police."

"How long before you have to go back overseas?"

"I'm not sure yet. I'll call the chief tomorrow. I hope to stay a couple of days to make sure Bri's really okay."

Then it would be roughly two months until she could see or kiss him again. "You could stay here. My bed's only a queen, but it'd just be the two of us this time." She moved close enough that they could touch.

"I wasn't sure you were ready for that yet."

Yet he'd stopped by here before going to his house. That seemed like a sign he'd at least thought about staying. She certainly hoped he had. Having spent so much time with him the past few days, she not only wanted to be intimate with him but trusted him enough to try.

"Honestly, I'm not one hundred percent sure, but I'd rather you stay than wait until you get back to find out." That way, if she wasn't ready, he had time to decide if he wanted to keep building on this or invest his time elsewhere. It would be better for her to know now than to set her heart on a relationship that wasn't going anywhere when the hurt would be another setback. She summoned one-hundred and ten percent of her courage to ask, "Do you have any condoms with you?" Now there'd be no doubt of her intentions.

"I've got at least one, probably two, with me. I'd like to stay but remember what I said." He wrapped an arm around her to hold her close as he spoke, looking right into her eyes. "If, at any time, you want to stop, you just say the word. Just don't say 'don't stop' because that can send mixed messages. I won't know if there's supposed to be punctuation between the words as in 'Don't. Stop!' or you're asking me *not* to stop. I don't want any miscommunication because I don't want to mess this up."

"Understood." Scenarios where she'd beg him not to stop made her mouth water. She could easily fall in love with Linc. In fact, she was already on her way there, and she so wanted this to work. "I'm afraid *I'll* be the one to mess things up."

"I don't see that happening. Tell me what you need."

She inhaled deeply and slowly exhaled. "I need to feel that *I* have control. And after watching you the past few days"

—and knowing his background in foster care—"I know how hard it is for you to not be in control."

"That's true. One of the things I like about the unit I serve with is having more control and input than being in regular army units. But I do have experience following orders. I'd be more than willing to take them from you."

"Any kind of order?" She traced a finger down his chest and stopped above the waistband of the black jeans that hugged his perfect body.

"As long as it's not anything illegal." His enticing grin amped up as he dropped his gaze to her hand. "And if control's what you need, you got it. You say where. No article of clothing comes off until you take it off or indicate you want me to. No blindfolds or flex cuffs—unless you want to use them on me. Not that I usually roll that way, but I'm willing if that makes you feel in control."

The idea of that, along with his smile, sent her body temperature skyrocketing. "I don't think we need to go that far." At least not yet. A prior fantasy or two flashed through her mind, though her body tensed at the idea of heading straight to the bedroom. "Why don't you get a little more comfortable by taking off your boots." She was already barefoot, and the suggestion gave her a few seconds to contemplate an appropriate starting place.

"Yes, ma'am."

She couldn't take her eyes off him as he braced one muscular arm against the wall and bent over to untie the laces. He toed off one low boot, then the other.

He held out a hand. When she placed hers in his, he interlaced their fingers but didn't move until she took the first step to the couch, where she sat in the middle.

"Your eyes are the most amazing color. Like honey ringed

with dark brown," he said. "They were the first thing I noticed about you. But they aren't your best feature."

"Oh?"

"I like your smile even better. And your heart. When we met at Bri's apartment, you built Bri up, telling her she could turn things around rather than bring up her past and mistakes. I was blown away, considering my experience with social workers started with Mrs. Courtland. She wasn't fazed by my or Bri's insistence that we stay together. She held me back as Regina loaded Bri in her car and drove away. And an hour later, she drove me to meet my first foster family, who already had three older boys."

"I'm sorry they couldn't keep you together, but your case worker might not have been the heartless person she came off as," Kendra shared. "In our line of work, we often don't have a choice. From what you said, Bri's grandmother was willing to take her in, and we always want to put children with family, if possible, but we can't *make them* take in family, much less non-blood relatives. She was probably doing her best for you, even if it wasn't what any of you wanted."

"You're probably right." He sighed. "I need to let that go, which will be easier now that I have a different take on social workers." He raised his eyebrows and leaned closer, tilting her chin with his index finger.

The simple touch sent electricity through her. Voltage amped up the moment his lips touched hers. Sweet kisses turned hotter and hotter. There was no doubt this man knew how to kiss.

When she tugged at his shirt, the back of her fingers connected with the warmth of his smooth skin, making her want to touch even more of him. To feel his skin against hers. "Take it off," she requested.

He stripped the shirt over his head in one fluid, sexy movement.

"I want to see the tattoo on your back."

He gave an almost bashful smile before he turned.

"Wolves." That wasn't what she'd expected. She ran her fingers over the most prominent one in the center with a serious, watchful gaze in its light eyes.

He looked over his shoulder at her. "I have the personality traits of a lone wolf. That's my nickname on the team."

A shiver of pleasure ran through her that he shared his nickname.

"It doesn't mean I'm dangerous. But I will protect my pack. I prefer small groups of people. Ones that I trust. I'm independent, and I don't like to need help."

"Um, hmm." She chuckled slightly at his admission.

"That middle one represents me," Linc said. "The smaller, pale colored wolf next to it is for Bri. I added it after she finished rehab. The pup is Jalen. I got that done after she decided to keep him, and I promised to help watch over him."

Her eyes misted as he explained. She touched a fingertip to the face of the two smaller wolves, then pressed her lips to the protector wolf.

"The ones in the background by the forest are for my team. They always have my back. How do you feel about tattoos?"

"I think this one fits you perfectly." Maybe one day he'd add a wolf for her. That'd be down the road, but she smiled at the idea.

He turned to face her again. She ran her hand from his shoulder, down the well-defined muscles of his arms, taking in the sight of his impressive abs before his mouth claimed hers.

She was in such a state of bliss that she offered no resistance when he maneuvered them to lay face to face and nose to nose and then lip to lip on the couch. His knee nudged between her legs.

It didn't take long before his thigh rose. His hand slid under her to the small of her back, applying pressure. When she writhed against his thigh, he ground harder. His solid erection pressed against her. She wanted Linc as much as she wanted her next breath.

Her fingers hesitated at the button to his pants, then trailed down the fabric covering the hard length of him, which pulsated against her palm.

A pleasured rumble rose from his chest into his throat.

Rather than shy away, she curved her palm to cup him. He leaned against her hand, rotating his hips while his smoldering, dark brown gaze maintained contact with hers.

Removing her hand, she raised her torso to lift her shirt. Now, it was his turn to stare.

He licked his lips before trailing one finger down her cheek, then her neck, and over the curve of her breast. His hand covered and caressed one breast before tweaking her nipple through the thin fabric. "You doing good?"

"Better than good." She reached behind her to unclasp her bra, then slowly eased the straps down her arms. Linc swallowed and licked his lips again as she laid back. "I'll let you do the honors."

"Okay. But I'm going to take my time." He graced her with that soulful smile, and she couldn't determine if that was to make her more comfortable or to make her beg him for more—which she was close to doing already.

Even though he had the strength to overpower her easily, Linc stayed true to his word and did not pressure her in any way. His relinquish of control also restored the confidence that Don had stolen from her and banished the anxiety that usually took hold at this stage of intimacy.

First, Linc kissed her jawline, moved down her neck to her collarbone, then focused on the swell of her breast. Anticipation built as his warm tongue slid under the loosened lace edge of her bra to wet her skin. Finally, his mouth traversed to cover the peak where his hot, moist breath warmed her through the fabric. When he bit lightly, her back arched up toward him. The hand sliding up her thigh stopped before reaching the place she so wanted him to touch.

His teeth clasped the lace edge of her bra cup and pulled it down to bare most of her breast. He removed the bra and tossed it to the floor. "Perfect."

The way he kissed and nibbled and sucked had her in no hurry to make him move on to the next step yet. She simply enjoyed as he focused on her pleasure and not his own in a way she'd never experienced. As he lavished equal attention on the other breast, her hand ran down the muscles of his arm to take his hand and guide it higher.

He obediently followed orders, first palming her, then his finger gently stroked before delving in to tease and explore. She pressed against his hand and clenched around his finger. After spending the past few days dreaming about Linc, his touch already had her on the brink of coming.

"Let's take this to the bedroom where there's more room," she said, her breathing labored.

"I like that idea." He eased off the couch to a standing position and extended his hand.

Inside the bedroom, Linc removed his wallet from his pocket. He opened it, then held up foil packages. "Two." He laid them on the nightstand while unfastening his pants with the other hand.

The way he said it and eyed her, she banked on them using both. She skimmed off her leggings as his pants dropped to the floor.

They both paused, taking in each other's bodies. His legs were muscular like the rest of him. That a man this amazingly fit and gorgeous was attracted to her had seemed too good to be true when he first asked her out. Since then, she'd lost some pounds and a dress size, but she was no stick figure. Her stomach certainly wasn't flat, and she needed an underwire bra to keep the girls perky, but Linc made her feel beautiful and desirable.

More than that, he listened, made her feel respected, and they worked together as a team. Other than his military service, they were compatible in all the ways that mattered— or at least they were about to find that out.

She turned down the spread and sheet. "You first."

Linc quickly dispatched his boxer briefs, giving her a good look at his impressive erection as he climbed onto the bed wearing only the half of a heart necklace that she wouldn't ask him to take off—another sign of his devotion to family. Her pulse pounded as she peeled off her panties and joined him. She'd never wanted a man this much. This was how she'd once dreamed it could be. No fear. Because everything about them together was right.

Raising her hand to her mouth, she licked her fingertips before circling his nipple.

"*Mmm.* I like that." He angled closer and kissed her, and his hand ran lazily up her side to fondle her breast.

Desire intensified as they took their time kissing and touching. Exploring and caressing. After she moistened her palm, thumb, and index finger, she slid her hand up and down his shaft and squeezed the head.

His throaty groan encouraged her.

"On your back," she ordered. Once again, he complied like a good soldier, and she scooted lower on the bed. She kissed his chest and circled his nipple with her tongue before lightly clamping it between her teeth.

One hand twisted into her hair. His other drifted down her back to her hip, and when he cupped her ass and nudged his knee between her legs, she straddled him. Despite Linc's strength, being on top gave her a sense of control.

His hips lifted off the bed, and she rocked against the steely hardness trapped under her core. Bending over, she suckled one dark nipple and then moved to the other.

"You keep doing that, and I won't last long." His fingers dug into her hips.

She lifted her head and smiled down at him, enjoying the power she held over him now. But it was time—past time.

Reaching over, she snagged a condom. "I'm not good at this." She handed him the package.

"I got it. You ready?"

"Definitely." She took his hand and guided it between her legs to show him just how ready she was.

He used her moisture to lubricate his shaft. Once he'd rolled on the condom, he stared into her eyes and gripped her hips as she took him in a little at a time, then raising up before taking him in fully as the most exquisitely pleasurable sensations overwhelmed her body.

His hands covered her breasts possessively, pinching and rolling her nipples between his fingertips, making her delirious with need. He thrust upward as she bore down. She ground her hips in a circle.

She rocked harder and faster as her muscles tightened, and she neared climax. Needing that last magic touch, she reached between them.

"Let me." Linc slid his hand under hers. His fingers expertly stroked their target, rubbing back and forth with the perfect amount of pressure that sent her over the brink.

Her head lolled back, and her lungs worked overtime to draw in oxygen. Linc raised his hips even higher as he joined her in riding out their intense orgasms.

Panting, her body sagged forward, and she collapsed onto him. She listened to his heartbeat as his chest rose with strained breaths and his fingers trailed lazy strokes over her lower back.

After several deep breaths, she lifted her head to kiss his jaw, then his mouth. "Thank you."

He chuckled, and the arm draped over her hugged her closer. "Anytime you want to be in control, just let me know."

"I might need a little time to recover my energy." She panted, still trying to catch her breath, as she shifted off him to lay at his side. "I was thinking next time, I'd let *you* be in control." She ran the back of her finger from his shoulder, along his side, to the inside of his thigh.

The wicked grin he gave her made her heart skip a beat in anticipation. Was it too soon to say I love you? Yes. Definitely.

There were things she loved about him. A lot of things. But she wouldn't drop the L word too soon and risk sending him running back to wherever he was deployed.

EITHER MOVEMENT or sound woke Kendra. She opened her eyes to see Linc pulling on his pants. His gaze roved over her, making her entire body heat from the memory of their second time making love last night—with him totally in control. And from behind, his hands had been free to roam and play her body as expertly as he did everything else.

"If I hadn't promised Bri I'd get Jalen, I'd stay right here with you," he said in that low, husky voice that further melted her insides. "There are things we could do that don't require condoms." He ran his tongue between his teeth suggestively before he leaned in to kiss her. "I could come back after I drop Jalen off at school."

"Tempting. However, my day is packed after being out of the office. This morning I'm meeting with a couple to finish their home study to become foster parents with the intention to adopt. I had to run out on them last Thursday when Jalen's school's director called me to pick him up."

Link stood straighter. "The ones you mentioned when you brought up putting Jalen in foster care?"

"Only because you asked about your chances of getting custody if something happened to Bri. I wasn't questioning your capability. I've seen you with Jalen. I have no doubts you'll be a great father."

"I may be a great *uncle*, but being a father is different. I could fill in short-term, but usually, I show up and spoil him. Bri is the one carrying the responsibility—making all the decisions, getting him to appointments, working to pay the bills."

"She's doing great, and I have no doubt you'd also be up to the challenge."

"I never had a role model to teach me how to be a father."

"It sounds like Bri didn't have much of a role model to be a mother, either. No one's perfect. We all make mistakes. Being a parent involves learning as you go."

"With my background, I decided years ago that marriage and family aren't for me."

His statement sucked the air out of her lungs along with the hope that had built over the past few days. "You're saying you don't want a wife and family?" It contradicted the behavior she'd witnessed the past few days.

"It's not my plan."

"Her lungs couldn't draw in a full breath with the weight lodged in her chest. Tears formed as she died a little inside.

"It's hard enough to maintain a marriage without throwing in constant deployments and reintegrations."

"But it can be done. Look at your friend, Walt."

"He's on his third marriage. Mack's on his second. And the risk of serving in Special Ops is high. I don't want to be responsible for kids growing up without both parents in their lives."

It sounded like a case of introjection and Linc expecting the worst outcome.

"Marriage and family is what you want, isn't it?" he asked.

"Yes." More than anything.

"I don't want to come between you and your family. With their feelings about you having a relationship with a military guy, I didn't think you'd want to take things further with me. I should have said something last night."

"It's not like we're at that point in a relationship to have that discussion." Even calling what they had a relationship was premature. She'd made assumptions based on what she'd seen in Linc with Jalen. And because it's what she wanted. "I don't regret what happened last night, but if we want different things, it's better to find that out now."

"True. I don't want to hurt you or waste your time."

"You didn't do either. In fact, you gave me a piece of myself back that I needed. But I can't make you change your mind. Staying in a relationship hoping things might be different wouldn't be fair to either of us. Not when I know that *is* what I want." That he'd made her face her past and helped her deal with her sexual assault made her push him this time. "If you think you can't have a wife and family because you aren't worthy or don't deserve it, then *you're* wrong. Think about that. Accept that you can't change the past but can move on and take control of your future. You may not see your worth, but *I* do. You deserve to have the things you want in life."

"Like I said, it's not in my plans. And I didn't mean to hurt or mislead you."

"I'll be fine." Maybe. After a few good cries and time. Except she didn't have time for that now. She'd bury herself in work for the next few days. When she came up for air, Linc would be gone. And take with him the temptation to reach out. Though she doubted he'd disappear from her thoughts as quickly as he would from her life.

IT WAS EERILY quiet inside Bri's apartment. Linc cracked open her bedroom door and let out the breath that had stalled in his lungs until he saw her and Jalen still sound asleep. Bri's arm protectively draped over Jalen's small frame.

"Hey J-man," Linc touched his arm. "Time to get ready for school."

"I want to stay with Mommy," he muttered sleepily and rubbed a fist to his eye.

"Mommy and Grams need to go do some work with Miss Clara this morning," Linc said, keeping his voice low. He coaxed Jalen from the bed and carried the clothes Bri had laid out for him to the living area.

While Jalen dressed and Linc assembled breakfast, Bri emerged from the bedroom.

"You didn't have to get up yet. I'll take him to school."

"I wanted to spend a few minutes with him." She sat on the kitchen chair and pulled Jalen onto her lap, playfully kissing the side of his head over and over.

His nephew's giggles lightened Linc's mood.

"Isn't that the same shirt you wore yesterday?" She eyed him as he poured the egg mixture into the pan.

"I overslept and grabbed the first thing I found so I wouldn't be late." That was mostly true.

"You? Late?" she scoffed.

"I've had a stressful few days worrying about you," he deflected. He wouldn't tell Bri he spent the night with Kendra —especially with how things ended. Pressure in his chest expanded. After what he'd overheard between Clara and Kendra about having kids at Malloy's house, he wanted to be upfront that his future didn't include marriage and kids, but when she'd invited him to spend the night, his honorable intentions got kicked to the curb. He couldn't wrap his head around her viewing him as both husband and father material when she knew everything about his background and family.

"I still can't believe you came." Bri's voice cracked.

"I would have come to Mexico if I'd known where to find you."

"I did envision you kicking in the door to save me. But, after they showed me the picture of Jalen on the playground at school, all I could think about was keeping him safe. Jalen said that and he and you and Kendra stayed at your friend Dev's house?"

"Seemed like the safest option. Tawnya's people knew where you lived. And she knew about me, and they could have found out where I lived. Malloy staked out the preschool. He even tailed Kendra after she picked Jalen up. We couldn't risk them tracking her down because she would know where Jalen was."

"Considering they kidnapped Grams, they probably would have gone after a child. Would they have really hurt them?"

"These people have no qualms about hurting others to

make money. You mean nothing to them. That's why authorities wanted whoever Tawnya worked for. You should be safe now." He set a plate of food in front of Jalen.

"Tawnya suckered me in. I thought she wanted a friend. I should have known she had an ulterior motive since the nearly free trip was too good to be true."

"Quit beating yourself up. They worked you."

"I was an easy target. I thought after all I've been through, I deserved something good to happen."

"You do deserve good things. You've stayed clean, and you're doing a fantastic job with Jalen. She's the best mom ever. Right, J-man?"

"Uh-huh," he agreed with his mouth full of food.

"I don't know about that, but I'm doing the best I can. I owe him that." She ran a hand over the back of her son's head. "I know I give you a hard time when you try to help, but I do appreciate it. I couldn't do this on my own."

Linc sat at the table and extended a hand to Bri. "You don't have to do it on your own. I wasn't there when we were kids, but I'm here now. Anytime."

"*You* need to let *that* go." She squeezed his hand. "It wasn't your fault. I never blamed you. And it would have happened again if you hadn't stuck to me afterward like we were conjoined twins."

Linc shrugged. It'd been the only way he'd known to protect her. They sat there while Jalen finished eating.

"Go brush your teeth. Uncle Linc will take you to school, but I'll pick you up." Bri lifted Jalen off her lap and watched him disappear into the bathroom. "I wouldn't trade him for anything, but I don't want to do it on my own forever. Do you think I'll ever find someone to love me enough to marry me and be a father to Jalen?"

"If that's what you want, you just need to find the right

guy. But you know he'll have to pass muster with me." Linc grinned at her.

"You've got single friends. Maybe you should set me up with someone that would 'pass muster' so I don't waste my time finding someone just to have you scare him off."

He raised an eyebrow at her but didn't take the bait. There were too many ways that could go wrong.

She huffed. "I went out with a customer at the dealership a few times. He was getting used to the idea I was a single mom, but when he learned I'd used drugs, that was too much baggage for him. He said his sister had dated some *loser* who did drugs."

"Ouch."

"He tried to recover, saying he wasn't implying that *I* was a loser." She rolled her eyes and picked at her fingernail. "His family went through a lot with his sister's ex. I understood that he worked in the family business and didn't want to jeopardize his role there if his parents disapproved. But, despite me being clean for nearly five years, he ended things."

Linc immediately thought of Kendra's family and her not wanting to risk their disapproval by dating a man in the military. But she'd agreed and even been thinking beyond the short term—until he killed that possibility an hour ago.

"I get that a lot of men aren't able to get past my background, but I think the fact I don't get child support may have been a factor too. Outside of marriage, some men don't want to support their kids, much less someone else's."

"If they think that way, that's not the caliber of man you want, and they don't deserve you."

"I know better than to settle like Mom did, but I want more kids. Jalen needs a brother or sister or two. And cousins." She leaned forward as she said it and gave him a challenging grin.

"Then your husband better have siblings who have kids."

"Why do you always blow off that suggestion? And don't try to blame it on your job because I'm not buying that bull crap." She moderated her language as Jalen emerged from the bathroom.

"Because I don't know what to do. I never had a father. No offense, but yours didn't count."

"It's not like I learned much from our mother or even from Grams. It was people like Mrs. Shannon. Parenting classes I took through DSS. And your boss's wife, Stephanie, who threw that baby shower for me. Not only did they supply me with clothes and diapers, but the women who came also wrote down parenting tips on cards. Simple things like 'never wake a sleeping baby' and 'ways to deal with a two-year-old's tantrums.' I've even learned from you." She poked a finger in Linc's chest.

"Me?"

"Yes. I have to be both mother and father. Sometimes I get jealous because, in *some* situations," she qualified, "you're better with Jalen than I am."

"I am not."

"Yes, you are. Maybe we didn't have role models growing up, but you've had them in the military. I envy your relationship with men like your Chief Lundgren."

He'd learned a lot from the chief and others regarding work. About responsibility. Leadership. About being a team player—*a family*.

"I don't tell you often enough how proud I am of the man that you are. You think you're not up to being a parent," she laughed. "What does that say about *my* qualifications? I may not be perfect, but counseling helped me learn that it's okay, and to stop negative self-talk. I learn as I go and try not to repeat the same mistakes. And I think I'm doing a pretty damn good job."

Jalen gasped. "Mommy swore." He waved a finger at her.

"I did. I'm sorry. But your uncle won't admit he's wrong. It's one of his faults." Bri got Jalen's lunch box from the refrigerator and loaded it into his camouflage backpack.

"*One* of my faults? What are the others?" Seeing his sister's spunky side return—even at his expense—made things feel normal after the stress of the past few days.

"You walk away at the first sign of rejection."

"Hey, I—"

"I get it. It's a defense mechanism—and healthier than what I did to be accepted and dull the pain. You knew the odds of passing that qualification course to join Special Ops. You worked your butt off, so you'd pass the first time because you didn't want to be 'rejected.' Now look at you. You're one of the best of the best. You're not perfect," she raised an eyebrow, "but any woman would be lucky to have you. And so would any child." She'd softened her tone. "But, be warned, your future wife will have to pass muster with *me.*" She winked.

"How many other faults do you want to expound on? Because I don't want Jalen to be late for school?" And he needed out of this conversation.

"We'll pick it up later."

Why had he given her that opening? "I'll be back to take you and Regina to the police station when you're ready." Linc hustled Jalen toward the door.

"Can we listen to Bluey music in the car?" Jalen asked.

"I don't have that kind of music on my playlist," Linc said.

"I'll send you my playlist of his favorite songs." Amusement laced Bri's voice. "You'll love it. 'Baby Shark' is on there and 'The Gummy Bear Song.'"

He'd try to remember to delete his play history later because he'd give this kid—and his sister—most anything they wanted.

TWENTY-ONE

Clara greeted them inside the police station. "Mrs. Feldman, Officer Logan will take your statement, and I'll take yours, Brianne."

"You can come with me," Officer Logan said politely and led Regina to his desk.

"Can I get you a cup of coffee or some water?" Clara asked.

"I could use some water." Bri twisted her hands together.

"I'll take a coffee." Linc touched Bri's upper back, hoping to calm her nerves.

Clara motioned for Linc to follow her as well. "We'll use this interview room for privacy." She opened the door to a room off the main squad room and motioned Bri in. "I'll grab the water. Since it's police station coffee, you can come with me and fix it how you want it," she said to Linc.

Once they were in the small break room, he poured a coffee and added creamer. "Thanks for not calling it an inter-rogation room."

"I'll assure her that she's not in any trouble." Clara

grabbed a water bottle from the fridge. "I take it everything went well with Kendra last night?"

Based on her grin and the innuendo in her voice, she knew, or at least suspected, he'd spent the night. However, she must not have talked to Kendra this morning and didn't know about their conversation ending their brief relationship, if you could call it that. He didn't ask or answer her question as he stirred the coffee.

"I don't think you'll have to worry about Grandma Ruby. You're going to change her mind, and she'll be asking you to set her up with some retired Special Forces soldier. When do you go back to finish out your deployment?"

"I'm going to call my chief and work that out while you're interviewing my sister. Can I trust you to stick to the case?" He didn't need Bri getting the lowdown on him and Kendra because Bri would probably give him hell.

"Of course." Clara's playful smile disappeared, and she studied him through the narrowed eyes of a skilled detective. "You can wait in the lobby after you make your call."

He gave a curt nod, then headed outside.

"I got your message," Chief Lundgren answered. "Glad to hear Bri's back safe, and they caught the people behind the operation."

Amen to that. "She and her grandmother are giving their statements to the police now. The detective working the case said neither should be in danger going forward. Her grandmother wants to go home to Atlanta tomorrow, except she's still recovering and not up to making the drive herself. Bri asked me to drive her down. I thought I could fly out of Atlanta back to Poland."

"It'll make it an easier trip for you. Call HQ and have them make arrangements. We're not doing more ordnance training until you're back. Our newbie or a trainee might get a nickname like three-finger G.I. Joe if I let Dominguez and Grant fill in for you."

"Our newbie have a nickname yet?"

"No. We wanted you to have a say."

The chief wanting him back and verbalizing what Linc brought to the team was what he needed to hear. Getting back to work might give him something to think about other than Kendra and wondering if he'd made a huge mistake this morning.

TWENTY-TWO

Linc removed the bag of coffee from the freezer to make a pot of strong brew. Despite being in his house and bed, he'd barely slept.

The fridge was as empty as the house felt after his time with Jalen and Kendra. She'd invaded his every thought. And it had only taken one night together and one alone to make him feel like something was missing from his life.

Since before dawn, he'd replayed her speech telling him she saw his worth over and over until it had started to drown out the negative messages repeated so many times in so many ways that he had believed them.

Shortly after her stint in rehab, Bri had told him how counseling helped shift her perspective from a victim mentality. She'd encouraged him to consider seeing a therapist to deal with any issues from their upbringing, but he'd blown off the suggestion. After all, he was a tough Spec Ops guy. His kind didn't need sympathy for having a crappy childhood or want to talk about their feelings.

What Bri said about him walking away at the first sign of rejection as a defense mechanism was true. What if, instead of protecting him from being hurt, it kept him from having the life he'd once dreamed of?

Jalen had stolen his heart the first time Linc held him as a newborn. Though he didn't plan to become a father, he loved being Uncle Linc. He thought back to what Kendra had said yesterday morning.

As a kid, he dreamed about being part of a functional family. His mom getting clean and making him and Bri her priority. That hadn't happened. But he'd still dreamed about one day having a wife who loved him. Having kids he'd love and protect. Except the fear he didn't deserve or wasn't good enough to take care of a family had been pounded into him over and over.

Most days, he risked his life serving in the military. The time had come to risk something else. He wanted to believe what Kendra said. That what she saw in him was true. He could have the life he'd dreamed of as a kid.

It was early. However, he only had four hours until he had to leave Fayetteville, so he pulled out his phone and scrolled through his contacts.

AFTER VERIFYING Kendra's car was in the DSS parking lot, Linc entered the building. He passed through security and made his way to the reception area.

"I need to see Kendra Andrews," he told the same middle-aged receptionist he remembered from his prior visit.

"Do you have an appointment?"

"I don't, but it's important that I speak to her for a few minutes."

"You were here last week, right?"

"I was, but this is personal business."

The receptionist gave a knowing smile. "I got you, dear." She picked up the phone. "Kendra, you have a visitor at the front desk. They need you to sign for something." She winked at Linc, then hung up. "She'll be right out."

Linc shifted his weight as he waited. The way Kendra froze in the hallway and her mouth hung open as she stared, made his heart stop beating. She regained her composure to meet him by the desk.

"I take it I don't need to sign anything." Kendra's gaze shifted from Linc to the receptionist.

The receptionist gave a guilty shrug. "I know you're busy playing catch-up, and he didn't have an appointment, but *I'd* want to see him if he asked for *me*." She batted her lashes.

"Is there someplace private we can talk?" he asked Kendra.

"I can see if either conference room is available," the receptionist offered.

"That's okay. We'll go outside." Kendra motioned him to exit.

Was she going to blow him off? His airway constricted, and a tightness spread from his chest to his gut, but he wasn't going to retreat, no matter what artillery she lobbed his way.

"How are Bri and Regina doing?" She remained standing rather than sit on one of the metal benches to the side of the entrance.

"They're good. Between the kidnapping charges, firing on a law enforcement officer, and the drugs, cash, and weapons found, Tawnya, Malloy, and their boss are going away even without them testifying, which is great news. Bri went back to work today. Regina wants to get home, but she's not comfortable driving to Atlanta yet. I think she wants to tell her friends in her book club and bridge group what she went through to get some sympathy, so I'm driving her to Atlanta today."

"You and Regina in a car for six hours? That sounds above the call of duty." The dawning of a smile and her light laugh eased the tension.

"Well, she's now referring to me as her step-grandson."

"It sounds like you two have made progress. When do you have to go back to Europe?"

"I fly out of Atlanta this evening. That's why I had to see you before I left. I've been thinking about what you said. A lot. I'm accepting that my upbringing impacted me more than I wanted to admit. You keep getting the message that you aren't worthy, and it sinks in."

She moved slightly closer and held out her hand. He took hold of hers. The electricity still there between them gave him hope he hadn't damaged this beyond repair.

"After Christmas, classmates would talk about the gifts they got from Santa. Mom barely had money for food or rent —and that was before drugs took priority over gifts. But the idea of Santa knowing who's been naughty and nice made me feel I wasn't as good as kids who got lots of great gifts. Regina taking in Bri, but not me, after Mom died reinforced that."

"I understand. I've seen similar situations play out. But it doesn't make it true."

"It wasn't a one-time thing. At the group home, we were enrolled in a program providing gifts for kids in foster care. They asked us to list what we wanted. We put down things like a gaming system and new sneakers. I said a bike so I could ride to see Bri. Instead, I got socks, underwear, a warm winter coat, and a basketball." Since he didn't play basketball anymore, his foster brother had traded him for a decent pair of sneakers he'd outgrown.

"I'm sure the family who had your name had good intentions. Often, good-hearted people think they know best. They don't stop to think that kids experiencing foster care want to be like their classmates and friends. Have the same kinds of things."

"Exactly. Then, there were the girls who didn't want to date a boy in the system. Or their parents didn't want them dating the child of an addict. That information gets out and spreads. It's hard to shake that kind of history."

"And while my family had similar experiences and wouldn't judge, the bias against military members was a trigger for you." She sighed with an apologetic expression.

He nodded. "Joining the military has been the best thing in my life. It's provided income, skills, routine, stability, and acceptance. It appealed to my sense of justice. Most of all, it gave me family. Maybe I didn't have a father figure growing up, but I've had mentors and role-models there. I need to get a few things straight in my head. This morning, I called a Green Beret friend. His wife is a counselor. We talked briefly, and she referred me to her colleague."

"That's a pretty major step."

"It is." It'd been hard to accept that he needed help, but it'd given him the courage to be here. He had to be willing to change. "But it's what I need to do if I'm going after the things I want in life, like a wife and kids. And I don't want just any wife. I want someone who gets me and isn't afraid to challenge me—or tell me my thinking is screwed up. If she's beautiful and compassionate, those are perks too." He took hold of her other hand. "I'm hoping you'll give me another shot. And that while I'm deployed, we can talk and message each other."

"I would like that. Very much." She closed the remaining distance between them. "I'm also willing to challenge Grandma Ruby. Because I'm not willing to settle for just any guy. I want someone who makes me feel the way you do. Safe. Protected. Respected. I get mushy inside watching you interact with Jalen. And you give me butterflies when you smile at me. Even more so when you kiss me. Which you should do right now."

He'd put his heart out there. This time, it hadn't been rejected. He happily followed Kendra's order to kiss the woman who instilled the required sense of worth to complete him.

TWENTY-THREE

Linc grabbed his rucksack the moment the plane stopped taxiing after landing at Fort Liberty.

"I don't think I've ever seen you as eager to get off the plane as today," Chief Lundgren said with his usual dry humor.

"This time is different." The two other times he had someone waiting to welcome him home from a deployment, he'd known it wouldn't be permanent. Tonight, Bri would be here with Jalen. More importantly, Kendra would be here.

His team all knew about their developing relationship. And so did Bri, who'd been surprised but happy and totally on board. Kendra's family also knew about them now.

Not surprisingly, Grandma Ruby had reiterated her opposition to military men. After Clara voiced her support, Ruby agreed to a video chat to meet. He survived Ruby's interrogation and was granted temporary approval, though he wouldn't get final judgment until they met in person. Between talking with Kendra almost daily and the weekly counseling sessions over the last two months, he had different plans for his future.

A future he now realized he deserved and could see with Kendra.

The honor of deboarding first defaulted to Mack Hanlon, who was eager to see his wife, daughters, and young son. The idea that one day he might be the first off for that reason was a new possibility—one that Linc liked.

As he made his way down the boarding stairs, he picked out the trio, madly waving to him. His heart filled with a sense of coming home like he'd never experienced. He didn't get a chance to read the colorful sign that Jalen held up before he bolted away from Bri, the sign flapping at his side.

"Uncle Linc! Uncle Linc!" Jalen's smile was contagious as he launched himself into the air. His little arms wrapped around Linc's neck and squeezed tight. He leaned back and placed a hand on each of Linc's cheeks. "I miss you, Uncle Linc."

"I missed you too, J-man." He gave him a light head butt. His gaze locked on the two women approaching, and he shifted Jalen to his left hip, and placed his arm around Bri's shoulders. He held her to his side and pressed a kiss to her temple.

"Welcome home, big brother." She wrapped her arms around the pair for a family hug.

"Good to see you." Two months ago, he feared he might never see Bri again. Instead, their relationship was as close now as when they were kids.

He deposited Jalen back into Bri's arms. Kendra moved closer, and he slipped an arm around her waist. "Hey, you."

"Hi."

"I'm glad you're here."

"I wouldn't have missed it. I've been waiting weeks for this." She tilted her face up.

He inhaled a scent like honeysuckle, pulling her warm,

soft body to his hard one. The first kisses were sweet, but it only took her slight murmur of pleasure to make him forget about everything but her.

"They're kissing a lot," Jalen said.

"I see that." Bri laughed.

Kendra broke the kiss and looked around bashfully as Dev approached the group.

"Hey there, J-man." Dev patted his arm, then addressed Bri. "I'm glad you're back home safely."

"Me too." She leaned her head to touch Jalen's. "Who's that?"

"That's the new guy," Dev answered.

Linc looked to follow Bri's gaze locked on Chief Lundgren and his wife talking with the newest—and single—Bad Karma team member. "Dev, this is Kendra." He made the introduction before Bri could get more information and start crushing on the newbie like she had with Dev. That had been a non-starter.

Kendra shook Dev's hand. "It's nice to meet you in person. I've heard a lot about you. Thank you for letting us crash at your house."

"No worries. I owed him for the renovation work he's been helping me with. Besides, we have to protect our future team member, the J-man. Show me that muscle," he teased and squeezed Jalen's bicep when he posed with his arm up. "We'll have to do dinner sometime."

"That sounds great," Kendra agreed.

"See you soon." Dev tapped fists with Linc, then Jalen, who added his standard explosion effect. Dev laughed and nodded to Bri and Kendra before moving off.

"Speaking of dinner, Bri and Jalen are joining us tonight for dinner at my place," Kendra said.

"If you eat all your mac and cheese, you get dessert," Jalen stated wearing a big smile.

Linc couldn't help but laugh. "Mac and cheese? That's my welcome home dinner? Hot dogs too?" He'd eat bologna with them if it was what Jalen wanted—provided Kendra was dessert.

"It's lobster mac and cheese for the adults, and filet mignon. No hot dogs tonight," Kendra promised.

"That sounds wonderful. Just Bri and Jalen? Not your whole family?"

"We'll wait at least a few days for that."

"I do want to meet them. Just not tonight." He liked the way Kendra's arm tightened around him possessively.

"There's time for that later. You earned bonus points with Grandma Ruby. She loved the shawl you sent for her birthday. She wore it to lunch with her friends and got several compliments."

"I'm not above bribery to win her over. I've been waiting to tell you something in person, not over the phone."

"Okay." She tilted her head to the side and gave him a hesitant smile.

He motioned to Bri to give him a minute and led Kendra a few steps away. "I want you to know that I am falling in love with you."

She gave him that smile he liked to think she reserved just for him. A smile that reached her eyes and into his heart. "Good. I've been working really hard to make that happen."

He laughed at her adoring expression. "It's definitely working."

"That's only fair since I'm falling, or may have already fallen, in love with you too."

"Is that so?" A woman saying that in the past had been the beginning of the end. Hearing it from Kendra was entirely different. Healing. Freeing. Validating. "Then my plan is working too."

"It is. I tried not to be swayed by the fact that you're incredibly attractive." She placed her palm on his chest. "But you made me let my guard down, seeing how great you are with kids." She slid her hand to cover his heart. "And then there was the whole being understanding and giving up control to me thing that I couldn't resist. I can't explain how much I looked forward to hearing from you these past two months. Even if it was only a text or a few minutes, or we couldn't talk about what happened that day."

"It was the highlight of my day too. Though there could be stretches on future deployments when I can't communicate regularly," he warned.

"We'll figure that out when the time comes. I thought you could stay with me tonight—since there's no food at your place." She wrinkled her nose playfully.

"Perfect." He liked her plan to give him time with Bri and Jalen. Then they could be alone. His gaze roved over her. "You look even more beautiful in person than on camera."

"Thank you." She batted her long lashes, drawing his attention from her glossy lips to her stunning eyes before dropping to the hint of cleavage, making him want to see more.

She'd clearly wanted to have this effect on him. "Food is not why I want to stay at your place."

"Good, because I have tomorrow off."

He liked the sound of that. He kissed her again, savoring the sweetness she had brought into his life. "I want to introduce you to the rest of my team."

Kendra gave him the courage to accept his value and worth despite his past. She filled that missing piece in his life, and he was looking forward to the future he now believed he deserved. There'd been many times in his life that he'd been left behind or felt like a cast-off. Not anymore. Maybe one day, they would tell their friends and kids they had drug smugglers to thank for bringing them together.

The End

Dear Reader,

Thank you for choosing *Complicated Past*. I hope you enjoyed Linc and Kendra's story. I enjoyed getting back to my Bad Karma Special Ops series. If you have not yet read the tastefully steamy Bad Karma Special Ops romantic suspense series, you can start with *Desperate Choices*, the prequel novella to the series. Then read *Deadly Aim*, *A Shot Worth Taking*, and *In the Wrong Sights*.

You can also get my novelette, *Undercover Angel*, which is Tony and Angela's backstory FREE by subscribing to my newsletter. If you like sweet with some heat romantic comedies, check out my Faking It series. Linc makes appearances in Faking it with the Bachelor and Faking it with the Green Beret.

Reviews and ratings are very much appreciated. Subscribe to my newsletter or social media to get updates of what's coming and when.

Happy reading.

ALSO BY TRACY BRODY

Sweet with some heat romantic comedies

Faking It Series

Faking it with the Bachelor

Faking it with the Green Beret

Not Faking it with the Colonel

Faking it for the Boss (December 2024)

Tastefully steamy romantic suspense

Bad Karma Special Ops Series

Desperate Choices (Prequel Novella)

Deadly Aim

A Shot Worth Taking

In the Wrong Sights

Complicated Past

Free Newsletter Subscriber Exclusive

Undercover Angel

Also available in the
Bad Karma Spec Op series

Faking It Series

Sweet (with some heat) Romantic Comedies

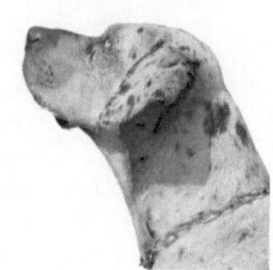

ACKNOWLEDGMENTS

To my incredible plot-fixer friend Paula Huffman, who blew up what I planned for this story and made it so much better. I loved making Linc struggle with being on his own and bringing out his softer side with his nephew.

I wanted to send the message to women that Linc delivers to Kendra that a woman has the right to say no regardless of how far things have gone because of friends who shared instances of guys pressuring them to engage in sexual acts and hearing how it still impacted them decades later. I hope that scene will give someone the courage to say no if she's not comfortable and maybe help some readers to get help if needed from similar situations in their past. You are not alone, and you didn't do anything wrong.

Thank you to Laura for your fabulous job with developmental insights and copy edits and working with my last-minute deadlines. I so appreciate it and you!

As always, a shout out to MSG Dale Simpson (US Army Ret.) for answer my calls, texts, and questions. I appreciate you and your sense of humor.

Thank you to our Armed Forces and their families for serving and sacrificing. You're my inspiration and heroes. And a shout out of thanks to Jeremy Lowe for your work with Home for the Troops and your generosity in bidding on my contribution in the auction. I hope your daughter is surprised and happy with her portrayal and role in the story.

Lastly, much thanks and love to my family for their support and patience, allowing me to do what I love.

ABOUT THE AUTHOR

Tracy Brody began writing spec movie and TV scripts, however, she switched to using her overactive imagination and sense of humor to write romance books. Her heroes all wear camouflage and her heroines aren't damsels waiting to be saved. She's published four tastefully-steamy romantic suspense books in the Bad Karma Special Ops series and four sweet-with-some-heat romantic comedies in her Faking It series.

Tracy invokes her sense of humor while volunteering at the USO. You may spot her dancing in the grocery store aisles or talking to herself as she plots books and scenes while walking in her neighborhood, the park, or at the beach.

Tracy enjoys hearing from readers. She'd love for you to connect with her. Sign up to get her monthly newsletter https://www.tracybrody.com/newsletter-signup

Join the fun in her private Facebook group Tracy's Team https://www.facebook.com/groups/tracyssfteam

amazon.com/Tracy-Brody/e/B083G9NHTL

facebook.com/tracybrodyauthor

instagram.com/tracybrodybooks

tiktok.com/@tracybrodybooks

goodreads.com/TracyBrodyBooks